D0065795

7-DAY
BOOK

Classics of Modern Science Fiction

THE PARADOX MEN

Volume 7

Books by Charles L. Harness

Flight Into Yesterday (1953)
(Revised as *The Paradox Men*, 1984)
The Rose (1966)
The Ring of Ritornel (1968)
Wolfhead (1978)
The Catalyst (1980)
Firebird (1981)
The Venetian Court (1982)

Classics of Modern Science Fiction

THE PARADOX MEN

CHARLES L. HARNESS

Volume 7

Introduction by George Zebrowski
Foreword by Isaac Asimov
Afterword by Brian Aldiss

Series Editor: George Zebrowski

Crown Publishers, Inc.
New York

Library of Congress Cataloging in Publication Data

Harness, Charles L.
  The paradox men.

  (Classics of modern science fiction; v. 7)
  I. Title. II. Series.
PS3558.A62476P3   1984   813'.54   84-5913
ISBN 0-517-55433-X
10 9 8 7 6 5 4 3 2 1
First Edition

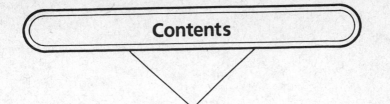

Contents

Retrieving the Lost

by Isaac Asimov

T HE HISTORY OF contemporary science fiction begins with the spring of 1926, when the first magazine ever to be devoted entirely to science fiction made its appearance. For a quarter-century thereafter science fiction continued to appear in magazines—and only in magazines.

They were wonderful days for those of us who lived through them, but there was a flaw. Magazines are, by their very nature, ephemeral. They are on the newsstands a month or two and are gone. A very few readers may save their issues, but they are fragile and do not stand much handling.

Beginning in 1950, science fiction in book form began to make its appearance, and some of the books retrieved the magazine short stories and serials in the form of collections, anthologies and novels. As time went on, however, it became clear that the vast majority of science-fiction books were in paperback form, and these, too, were ephemeral. Their stay on the newsstands is not entirely calendar-bound, and they can withstand a bit more handling than periodicals can—but paperbacks tend to be, like magazines, throwaway items.

That leaves the hardback book, which finds its way into public libraries as well as private homes, and which is dura-

ble. Even there, we have deficiencies. The relatively few science-fiction books that appear in hardback usually appear in
small printings and few, if any, reprintings. Out-of-print is
the usual fate, and often a not very long delayed one, at that.

Some science-fiction books have endured, remaining
available in hardcover form for years, even decades, and appearing in repeated paperback reincarnations. We all know
which these are because, by enduring, they have come to be
read by millions, including you and me.

It is, of course, easy to argue that the test of time and
popularity has succeeded in separating the gold from the
dross, and that we have with us all the science-fiction books
that have deserved to endure.

That, however, is too easy a dismissal. It is an interesting and convenient theory, but the world of human affairs is
far too complex to fit into theories, especially convenient
ones. It sometimes takes time to recognize quality, and the
time required is sometimes longer than the visible existence
of a particular book. That the quality of a book is not recog-
nizable at once need not be a sign of deficiency, but rather a
sign of subtlety. It is not being particularly paradoxical to
point out that a book may be, in some cases, too good to be
immediately popular. And then, thanks to the mechanics of
literary ephemerality, realization of the fact may come too
late.

Or must it?

Suppose there are dedicated and thoughtful writers and
scholars like George Zebrowski and Martin H. Greenberg,
who have been reading science fiction intensively, and with
educated taste, for decades. And suppose there is a publisher
such as Crown Publishers, Inc., which is interested in providing a second chance for quality science fiction which was
undervalued the first time round.

In that case we end up with Crown's *Classics of Modern Science Fiction* in which the lost is retrieved, the un-
justly forgotten is remembered, and the undervalued is
resurrected. And you are holding a sample in your hand.

Naturally, the revival of these classics will benefit the publisher, the editors, and the writers, but that is almost by the way. The real beneficiaries will be the readers, among whom the older are likely to taste again delicacies they had all but forgotten, while the younger will encounter delights of whose existence they were unaware.

Read—
And enjoy.

Introduction

by George Zebrowski

READER, YOU HOLD in your hands one of the most unusual science-fiction novels ever published. A shorter magazine version appeared in the May 1949 *Startling Stories* under the title *Flight Into Yesterday*. A badly edited, poorly proofread and printed hardcover was published in 1953 under the same title, with the text somewhat expanded. An Ace Double Novel (D-118) paperback was released in 1955 as *The Paradox Men*. And then the novel went out of print in the United States.

There was a renewed interest in Harness's work during the 1960s, begun by editor Michael Moorcock in the pages of *New Worlds*. Faber published a new edition of *The Paradox Men* in 1964, with a glowing introduction by Brian Aldiss. A British book club edition appeared in 1966, and a paperback in 1967. In 1976 Brian Aldiss and Harry Harrison reintroduced the novel to British readers in their limited edition SF Masters Series, published by New English Library. But there was no new American edition.

Harness's most famous work, *The Rose* (written during the first five years of a career that began with "Time Trap" in the August 1948 issue of *Astounding Science Fiction*) had failed to find an American publisher. The novel appeared finally in the British magazine *Authentic Science*

Fiction for March 1953. With the renewed interest in Harness's work, a British paperback was published in 1966, was followed by a Sidgwick & Jackson hardcover in 1968, and finally an American paperback came out from Berkley (X1648) in 1969. The British Panther paperback of 1969 was reprinted in 1970 and 1981. According to the author, none of these editions is the complete book, which he cut for its magazine appearance.

But there was still no new American edition of *The Paradox Men*, even though Brian Aldiss had intrigued younger readers by reprinting a chapter from the novel in his wonderful retrospective anthology *Space Opera* (Doubleday, 1974). Critics, editors, and reviewers had, from time to time, whet readers' appetites by mentioning this legendary book. In his note to the reprint of Harness's first story, "Time Trap," in *Alpha One* (the first volume of a distinguished retrospective anthology series begun by Ballantine in 1970), editor Robert Silverberg called *The Paradox Men* "a dizzyingly intricate novel, which repays close study by anyone wishing to master the craft of plotting." William D. Vernon, writing as recently as 1981 in *The Science Fiction Collector*, laments that "this is a novel not to be missed, if the reader can locate a copy." In the same issue of this publication Vernon presents an illustrated and annotated bibliography of Harness's short stories, novelettes, novellas, and novels, clearly demonstrating the author's substantial contribution to science fiction; but still no publisher took the cue to do a new edition of *The Paradox Men*.

Harness's original title for this novel was *Toynbee Twenty-two*, which refers to the famous British historian's numbering of civilizations that have come and gone. T-21 is the number of the civilization in the story, which is trying to avoid decline. Certain Toynbeean philosophers and other individuals of Harness's world hope that space travel (by means of a faster-than-light Starship, the T-22) will serve as a bridge to a new culture. Interestingly, our own world also harbors the hope that the opening of space will liberate human hearts and minds, as we move beyond a planet of limited economic horizons into an open universe.

Flight Into Yesterday, the magazine and hardcover title of this novel, was chosen by Sam Merwin, then editor of *Startling Stories*. *The Paradox Men* was the title Donald A. Wollheim gave to the Ace paperback. It is perhaps the most intriguing of the novel's three titles and describes accurately the ambiguous predicament of the novel's main characters. It is for this last reason, and to avoid confusing readers and bibliographers, that we have chosen the title given to the novel's largest previous edition. Also, the author has given the novel a careful line by line editing, correcting dropped punctuation, typos, wrong words, and taking the opportunity to expand overly compressed scenes, as well as tightening the reader's understanding of important details and improving the general movement of the story. It is my view that the purely mechanical defects of previous editions made the novel needlessly harder to read. In other words, this new edition of *The Paradox Men* has been given the normal book editing that was uncommon in the science-fiction field back in the forties and fifties. This edition, with some three thousand five-hundred words of added and revised material, is therefore the first definitive version of a genuine science-fiction classic, and replaces all previous editions.

The response of reviewers and critics in the year following the book's publication was mixed. Groff Conklin, writing in *Galaxy*'s January 1954 issue, seemed baffled by the novel—but he found it "pretty astonishing, if only because of the cauldronful of ideas and fantasies that are mixed up in it." P. Schuyler Miller, in the April 1954 *Astounding Science Fiction*, found the novel to be an "action entertainment" of some interest, but he failed to convey anything of the book's compulsive, dreamlike power. Anthony Boucher, writing in the September 1953 issue of *The Magazine of Fantasy and Science Fiction* described the story as a "fine swashbuckling adventure of space-and-time travel, the palace politics of tyranny, and the identity-problems of an amnesiac superman . . ." and compared it to A. E. Van Vogt's well-known "Weapons Shop" novels; but in the end Boucher found Harness's story too intricate, its science confusing and perhaps mistaken. Only Damon Knight seemed to have noticed that this novel "represents the brilliant peak of Charles L. Harness's published work." He described the novel as being "symmetrically arranged, the loose ends tucked in, and every last outrageous twist of the plot fully justified both in science and in logic." (The review is reprinted in Knight's collected essays on science fiction, *In Search of Wonder*, 2nd edition, Chicago, 1967). "You can trust Harness," Knight continues, "to wind up this whole ultracomplicated structure, somehow, symmetrically and without fakery. Finally, when it's all done, the story means something. Harness's theme is the triumph of spirit over flesh. . . . This is the rock under all Harness's hypnotic cat's-cradle of invention—faith in the spirit, the denial of pain, the affirmation of eternal life."

Alar the Thief is pushed (by a hidden player) through a series of escalating experiences which develop his hidden nature and move him toward death and transfiguration—all in the cause of raising humankind out of its cul-de-sac of cyclic history. Harness's concern is with the unsatisfactory state of human nature, and many of his protagonists seek to transcend this fallen state. It is this theme that gives his stories their mythic overtones, while the scientific and technological ideas create a poetry of glittering plausibility. The casual reader will find a striking action story, but the lucky rereader will find epic poetry, an ecstasy of ideas, and a critical view of his own humanity.

Building on the pioneering, dreamlike scenarios of A. E. Van Vogt, Harness produced a more coherent and yet still emotionally satisfying version of the master's wheels-within-wheels story. *The Paradox Men* is comparable to Alfred Bester's *The Demolished Man* (1953) and *The Stars My*

Destination (1957) in its sweep and color, especially in the ethereal beauty of its closing pages. *The Stars My Destination* came later, however, and there even seems to be a bit of Harness in Kurt Vonnegut's *The Sirens of Titan* (1959), both of which are counted as among the finest modern science-fiction novels. Alar the Thief is kindred to Winston Niles Rumfoord; both characters are scattered across time, and both are trying to deal with a recalcitrant human nature, though Alar seems more ethical than the nihilistic Rumfoord. Aldiss, in his introduction to the first British hardcover, observes that "for all its slam-bang action, *The Paradox Men* holds a particular enchantment. I have likened it to novels I admire, *The Stars My Destination* (*Tiger! Tiger!* in Britain) and *The Sirens of Titan*; but they lack the tenderness for humanity that gives the present book its freshness and its last scenes their conviction. Unlike most of the science fiction being written in England, America, and Russia, the values here are not purely materialist." To this I can only add that no science-fictional hero ever reformed human history as thoroughly and as movingly as Alar the Thief; he steals the way to human progress. You'll have to read the novel to see what that means, but I promise you it will be worth the trip.

Classics of Modern Science Fiction

THE PARADOX MEN

Volume 7

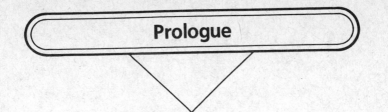

Prologue

He had not the faintest idea who he was.

And he didn't know why he was treading the cold black water so desperately.

He didn't know either why a great battered shining thing was sliding into the moonlit waves a dozen yards in front of him.

A vision of vast distances traversed at unimaginable velocities flicked across his numbed understanding but was instantly gone again.

His head ached horribly and he had no memory of anything.

Suddenly a blinding shaft of light swept the waters ahead of him and came to rest on the broken flank of the rapidly sinking wreckage. Along the top of the broken hull he thought he could see a tiny, great-eyed animal whose fur was plastered to its shivering sides.

Almost immediately a sleek, brass-trimmed boat whirled to a halt beside the fast-disappearing hulk, and he knew, without knowing why he knew, that he must not linger. Making sure that the thing he clasped in his left hand was safe, he turned toward the distant river shore lights and began a slow, silent breast stroke. . . .

Noose for a Psychologist

1

MASKED EYES PEERED through the semi-darkness of the room.

Beyond the metal door ahead lay the jewels of the House of Shey—a scintillating pile that would buy the freedom of four hundred men. A misstep at this point would bring hell down about him. Yet, in the great city outside, dawn was breaking and he must act quickly. He must tiptoe to the door, hold the tiny voice-box to the center of the great bronze rosette, pillage a fortune and vanish.

The slender black-clad figure leaned against the gold-and-platinum-tapestried wall and listened intently, first to the tempo of his strange heart, and then to the world about him.

From across the room, some six meters away, rose and fell the faint, complacent snoring of Count Shey, sometime Imperial Psychologist, but famed more for his wealth and dilettantism. His ample stomach was doubtless finishing off pheasant and 2127 burgundy.

Below his mask, Alar's lip curled humorlessly.

Through the doorway behind him he detected the rattle of a card deck and muffled voices—a roomful of Shey's personal guards. Not broken-spirited slave servants, but hard-bitten overpaid soldiers of fortune with lightning rapiers.

His hand tightened subconsciously on the hilt of his own saber and his breathing came faster. Even a trained Thief such as he was no match for six of the guards that Shey's fortune could afford. Alar had been living on borrowed time for several years and he was glad this assignment was dry-blade.

He glided with catlike silence to the bronze door, drawing the little cube from his waist-pouch as he did so. With sensitive fingers he found the center of the rosette with its concealed voice-lock. Pressing the cube to the cold metallic cluster, he heard a faint click, then the shrill recorded words, almost inaudible, of Shey, stolen from him, one by one, day by day, over the past weeks.

He replaced the cube in his waist-pouch and waited. Nothing happened.

For a long moment Alar stood motionless. Perspiration began to gather in his armpits and his throat grew dry.

Either the Society had given him an outdated voice key, or there was an additional, unaccounted-for variable.

And it was then that he noticed two things. The first was an ominous quiet in hall and guardroom. The second was that the gentle snores from the bed had ceased. The next moment stretched endlessly toward its breaking point.

His incorrect signal had evidently activated some unseen alarm. Even as his mind raced in frantic fury he visualized briefly the hard alert faces of half a thousand Imperial Police, who would be wheeling patrol jets about, then hurtling toward the area.

A faint hesitant scrape of sandals came from the hall. He instantly understood that the guards were puzzled, uncertain as to whether their entry would endanger their master.

He knew that soon one of them would call out.

In a bound he was at the bedroom door that opened to the guard annex and slammed it noisily behind electronic bolts. He listened momentarily to the angry voices on the other side.

"Bring a beam-cutter!" came a cry.

The door would be down in short order.

Simultaneously a heavy blow struck him in the left shoulder and the bedroom sparkled with sudden light. He whirled, crouching, and appraised coolly the man in bed who had shot him.

Shey's voice was a strange mixture of sleepiness, alarm and indignation. "A Thief!" he cried, tossing the gun away as he realized that lead-throwers were no good against a Thief's body-screen. "And I have no blade here." He licked pudgy lips. "Remember," he giggled nervously, "your Thief code forbids injuring an unarmed man. My purse is on the perfume table."

Both men listened to the blend of distant police sirens and the muffled curses and grunts coming from beyond the bedroom door.

"You will open the jewel room," said Alar flatly.

Shey's eyes widened.

"My jewels!" he gasped. "You shall not have them!"

Three sirens sounded very close. As Alar listened one of them choked off suddenly. I.P.'s would be swarming out of a patrol jet and setting up semiportable Kades in the street, capable of volatilizing him, armor or no armor.

The bedroom door was beginning to vibrate in resonance with the beam-cutter.

Alar strode almost casually to the bed and stood over Shey's heavy face, which was upturned in trembling pallor. In a startling snakelike movement the Thief seized his host's left eyelid between thumb and forefinger.

Shey chuckled horridly, then raised his head painfully and reluctantly. He found himself sitting on the edge of his bed, then standing beside it. And when he attempted to grasp the slender throat of his tormentor, a knife seemed to stab into his eyeball.

Sweat was pouring down his face when, a moment later, he stood before his beloved treasure room.

All the sirens had ceased wailing. A hundred or more jets must be waiting for him outside.

And Shey knew it too.

A cunning grin stole over the psychologist's mouth.

"Don't hurt me any more," he giggled. "I'll open the jewel room."

He put his lips to the rosette and whispered a few words. The door rolled noiselessly into the wall.

He staggered back and rubbed his eye gingerly as the Thief leaped into the treasure alcove.

With methodical speed Alar tore open the teakwood drawers and scooped their glittering contents into his pouch. A less experienced Thief would not have known where or when to stop but Alar, even in the act of reaching for a beautiful choker worth forty men, jerked back his hand and drew his pouchthong tight in a single motion.

He was at the portal in a bound, just in time to see the bedroom door crash inward beneath a dazzling mass of rapiers. Even as his own blade whipped from its scabbard and disarmed the foremost guard, he knew that the odds were too great, that he must be wounded and perhaps killed before he could leap from the mile-high window. This was so because, before he could leap, he must tie his coiled shock-cord to some immovable object. But to what? Shey's bed was no antique. It had no bedposts. Suddenly he knew the answer.

By a miraculous coordination of concentration and skill he had remained unscathed during his retreat to the open window. The guards, unaccustomed to such mass attacks on a single opponent, were thrusting ad lib instead of simultaneously and he was able to parry each thrust as it came. But now, probably by accident, two guards lashed at him from either side. He attempted an intricate level-blade parry for both thrusts, but the angle of approach of the two rapiers was too wide.

However, even as his blade was losing contact with that of the guard on his right, his left hand was drawing a noose of shock cord from the coil case on his chest, and as the blade seared into his side, he was throwing, left handed, a lasso towards the wet, balding face of Shey, who was crouching on the other side of the bed.

And then the Thief, without waiting to see whether the noose had seized Shey's neck, flung himself backward. The sword in his side did not pull free. Instead it was wrenched from the startled guard's hand. With the sword imbedded in his side, Alar plunged out of the window into space.

Somewhere in the first thirty meters, while he counted off the quarter seconds, he felt his side. The wound was not bad. The blade had sliced the flesh, was held now by his clothing. He tore the sword from his side.

The line would gradually grow taut at the fourth second, assuming that the noose had tightened about Shey's neck and that all the guards would be grasping at it with their bare hands for the better part of a minute before one of them should have the presence of mind to sever it with his sword. And by that time Alar would have cut it himself.

He suddenly realized that the whirling, crashing fifth second had come and gone, and that he was now plummeting in free fall.

The noose had not caught.

He noted almost curiously that he was beyond panic and fear. He had often wondered how death would come, and how he would meet it. He would not live to tell his companion Thieves that his reaction to imminent death was simply a highly intensified observation, that he could see individual grains of quartz, feldspar, and mica in the granite blocks of the wall of the great building as it hurtled up and past. And that everything that had happened to him in his second life flashed before him in almost painful clarity. Everything, that is, except the key to his identity.

For Alar did not know who he was.

As the mill of death ground away he relived the moment when the two professors had found him, a young man of about thirty. They had found him wandering adaze along a bank of the upper Ohio River.

He relived their searching tests of those far-off days. They were sure at the time that he was a spy planted by the Imperial Police, and for all he knew he might have been. His amnesia had been complete. Nothing of his past life had seeped through to suggest to him—or to his two new friends—what he might have been.

He remembered their astonishment at his voracity for knowledge, recalled in detail the first and last university class he had attended and how he had fallen into a polite doze after the instructor's fourth inaccuracy.

He remembered vividly how the professors, after they had finally become convinced that his amnesia was unfeigned, had bought false indicia of his educational history. With the papers, he became, overnight, a Doctor of Astrophysics on sabbatical leave from the University of Kharkov and a substitute lecturer at the Imperial University, where the two professors taught.

Then came the long walks at night, his arrest and beating by Imperial Police, his growing awareness of the wretchedness about him.

Finally, he saw the foul-smelling battered van clatter through the streets in the early morning with its wailing burden of aged slaves.

"Where were they being taken?" he had asked the professors later. "When a slave is too old to work he is sold," was all he could get from them.

But he had finally discovered the secret. The charnelhouse. The cost had been two bullets in his shoulder from the guard.

Of all nights that he could remember that was the most revelatory. The two professors and a third man, a stranger with a black bag, were waiting for him when he crept blindly into his room in the early morning. He recalled vaguely the painful probings in his shoulder, the white bandages and finally the momentary nausea that followed the flow of something tingling from his scalp to his toes—Thief armor.

By day he had lectured on astrophysics. By night he had learned the gentle arts of climbing a smooth wall with his fingernails—of running a hundred yards in eight seconds—of disarming three lunging Imperials. In his five years as a member of the Society of Thieves he had looted the wealth of Croesus, and the Society had freed tens of thousands of slaves with it.

Thus had Alar become a Thief, thus was he now fulfilling an unpleasant maxim of the Society of Thieves—No Thief dies a natural death.

Suddenly he felt a blasting blow on his back that tore his black vest off, and he realized that the shock cord, now tight as a steel wire, had jerked him back against the building.

His lungs filled to the bursting point in the first breath he had drawn during the fall.

He would live.

His descent was gradually being broken. The noose must have caught on Shey, after all. He smiled at the struggle that must now be going on far above him—six burly men holding a thread-like cord with their bare hands to keep their source of revenue alive. But within a matter of seconds one of them would think to cut the cord.

He looked below. He had not fallen as far as he had thought. It was now evident that he had counted the quarter seconds too rapidly. Why did time linger so in the presence of death?

Now the dimly-lit street was rushing up to meet him. Tiny lights scurried around below, probably I.P. armored cars with short-range semi-portable Kades as well as shell-throwers. He was certain that half a dozen infrared beams were bathing this side of the building, and knew that it was just a question of time before he was spotted. He doubted that the I.P.'s could score a direct shell hit on his body, but the shock cord was highly vulnerable. A flying metal fragment could easily sever it.

The lights below were now forbiddingly large. Alar lifted his hand to the cord case, ready to engage the decelerator. About one hundred feet above the ground he jammed home the gear lever and almost blacked out under the abrupt deceleration. And then he was stumbling dizzily to his feet, cutting the cord and starting up a street barely alight with the fast-coming dawn.

Which way to run? Would police cars with Kades guns be waiting for him when he turned the corner? Were all the streets blocked?

The next few seconds would have to be played very accurately.

A shaft of light stabbed at him from the left, followed by the stamp of running feet. He whirled in alarm to see a glittering sedan chair carried on the shoulders of eight stalwart slaves, whose sweating faces reflected the growing redness in the east. A woman's slurred voice floated to him, and then the chair was past.

Despite his growing peril he almost laughed. Now that nuclear-powered jet cars were available to all, the carousing nobility could distinguish themselves from the carousing bourgeois only by a return to the sedan chair of the Middle Ages. The padding feet died away.

Then, the shock of what she had said hit him. "The corner to your left, Thief."

The Society must have sent her. But he really had no choice. He swallowed hard and ran around the corner—and stopped.

Three Kades guns immediately swiveled in three I.P. cars to cover him. He three up his hands and walked slowly towards the car on the left.

"Don't shoot!" he cried. "I surrender!"

He gulped with relief as Dr. Haven dismounted from the impostor car, rapier drawn, and pretended to advance cautiously to meet him. A pair of handcuffs was gripped in one hand.

"The reward goes three ways!" called an I.P. from the middle car.

Dr. Haven did not turn, but held up a hand in acknowledgment.

"Easy, boy," he whispered to Alar. "Thank the gods you came this way. Lost a bit of blood? Surgeon in the car. Can you make it to your lecture?"

"I think so, but in case I pass out, the jewels are in my pouch."

"Beautiful. That gives us four hundred freemen." He seized Alar by the belt roughly. "Come on, you scum! You've got a lot of questions to answer before you die!"

A few minutes later the Thief car lost its escorts, changed its insignia and sped toward the University.

THE WOMAN SAT before the mirror, quietly brushing her black hair. Under the glow of the vanity lamp, the long strands were lustrous and fine, shimmering with blue highlights. The thick richness of her hair was a striking frame for her face, accentuating the whiteness of her skin, the cheeks and lips that were barely pink. It was a face as calm and cold as the hair was vibrant and warm. But the eyes were different. They were large and black and brought the face alive to harmonize with the hair. They, too, sparkled in the glow of the lamp. She could not dull those eyes as she could her face. She could only mask them, partially, by keeping her dark lashes low. She was keeping her eyes that way now, for the benefit of the man who stood behind her.

"You might be interested to learn of the latest offer," Haze-Gaunt said. He seemed to be toying idly with the emerald tassels on the vanity lamp, but she knew his every sense was strained to catch her faintest reaction. "Shey offered me two billion for you yesterday."

A few years ago she might have shuddered. But now . . . she continued to brush her black hair with long even strokes, and her quiet black eyes sought out his face in the vanity mirror.

The face of the Chancellor of America Imperial was like no other face on earth. The skull was smooth-shaven, but the incipient hairline revealed a broad high forehead beneath which were sunk hard intelligent eyes. The pupils were dark, immense. The aquiline nose showed a slight irregularity, as though it had once been broken and reset.

The man's cheeks were broad, but the flesh was tight-fitting, lean and scarless except for one barely visible cicatrix across the jutting chin. She knew his dueling philosophy. Enemies should be disposed of cleanly and without unnecessary risk, by specialists in the art. He was courageous but not naïve.

The mouth, she decided, might have been described in another man as firm; on him, however, it seemed vaguely petulant. It betrayed the man who had everything—and nothing.

But perhaps the most remarkable thing about him was the tiny, huge-eyed ape-thing that crouched in eternal fright on the man's shoulder, and which seemed to understand everything that was said. The warlock and his familiar, thought Keiris. What grotesque affinity had joined them?

Unsmiling, Haze-Gaunt asked, "You aren't interested?" He lifted his hand in an unconscious gesture and stroked his shrinking little pet.

He never smiled. Only a few times had she known him to frown. An iron discipline defended his face from what he seemed to regard as puerile emotional vanities. And yet he could never hide his feelings from her.

"Naturally, Bern, I'm interested. Have you entered a binding agreement for my disposal?"

If he was rebuffed, he gave no sign of it beyond an imperceptible hardening of his jaw muscles. But she knew he would have liked to rip the jeweled tassel from its enchased foundation and hurl it across the room.

She continued to brush her hair in unperturbed silence, her expressionless eyes looking calmly at his mirrored ones.

He said, "I understand that you called to a man on the

street early this morning when the chair slaves were bringing you in."

"Did I? I don't remember. Perhaps I was drunk."

"Some day," he murmured, "I really shall sell you to Shey. He loves to experiment. I wonder what he would do to you?"

"If you want to sell me, then sell me."

His mouth barely curled. "Not yet. You are, after all, my wife." He said it unfeelingly, but there was that faint trace of a sneer at the corner of his lips.

"Am I?" She felt her face grow warm and saw in the mirror the deepening shade of pink on her cheeks surging toward her ears. "I thought I was your slave."

Haze-Gaunt's eyes flickered in the mirror. He had noticed the flush of color on her skin, and she secretly raged that he did. These were his moments of satisfaction against her husband—her true husband.

"It's the same thing, isn't it?" he said. The faint sneer had subtly altered into a faint smirk.

She was right: he had scored and found his pleasure. She tried to twist the direction of the conversation. "Why bother to mention Shey's offer? I know I afford you far too much pleasure to exchange for a bit more wealth. More money won't satisfy your hatred."

The curl in his lips faded away, leaving only the sharp line of his mouth. His eyes locked with hers in the mirror.

"There is no one I need hate now," he replied.

What he said was true, she knew, but it was an evasive truth. He did not need to hate her husband, for he had destroyed her husband. He did not need to hate, but he still did. His bitter hatred and envy of the achievements of the man she loved was as strong as ever. It would never be quenched. That was why she was enslaved. She had been the beloved of the man he hated—she was a means for revenge against the dead.

"That has always been true," she said, holding his gaze steadily with her own.

"There is no one," he repeated slowly, "I need hate now." He bore down on the final word just enough for her to catch the stress. "You cannot escape the fact that I have you."

She deliberately made no reply. Instead she lazily shifted the brush from one hand to the other, attempting to make the movement an insolent gesture. She told herself, "You think I cannot escape, that I remain with you because I must. How little you know, Haze-Gaunt!"

"Some day," he muttered, "I really shall sell you to Shey."

"You said that before."

"I want you to know that I mean it."

"Do it any time you like."

The curl came back to his lips. "I will. But not yet. All things in due time."

"Just as you say, Bern."

The televizor buzzed. Haze-Gaunt bent over, snapped the "Incoming" switch and was welcomed immediately by a nervous giggle. The screen, in the intimacy of the boudoir, had a manually operated button which required continuous fingertip pressure for a two-way image. Haze-Gaunt thumbed the button. The screen remained blank.

"Ah," said the caller's voice, followed by some throat clearing. "Bern!" It was Shey.

"Well, well. Count Shey." Haze-Gaunt glanced at the woman. She had dropped the brush to her lap and straightened her dressing gown as he had reached for the switch. "Perhaps he's calling to increase his already generous offer for you, Keiris. But I will remain firm."

Keiris said nothing. Shey, at the other end, was making some querulous croaks, more over the unexpected greeting, probably, than from embarrassment. She knew, however, the subtle point behind Haze-Gaunt's remark. It served more than merely to drive another barb into her; Shey had been informed that she was present and, therefore, to be discreet.

"Well, now, Shey," Haze-Gaunt said abruptly. "What prompts your call?"

"I had an unfortunate encounter during the night."

"Yes?"

"With a Thief." Shey paused for the dramatic effect of his words, but Keiris noticed that there wasn't a flicker of a muscle in the face of the Imperial chancellor. His only reaction was a series of quick, rough strokes across the fur of the little animal on his shoulder. The tiny ape-thing shivered, wild-eyed, more frightened than ever.

"My throat was lacerated," Shey continued, when it became obvious that no comment was forthcoming. "My personal physician has been administering to me all morning." There was a sigh. "Nothing serious, no interesting pain, just soreness. And, of course, some bandages which only serve to make me look ridiculous." There was the reason, thought Keiris with secret amusement, for the blank screen—Shey's vanity.

The details of the attack and escape by the Thief came out swiftly. Plainly Shey's throat had recovered enough not to hamper his smooth flow of words. He concluded his narration by asking the chancellor to be sure to meet him a little later in the Room of the Meganet Mind.

"Very well," agreed Haze-Gaunt and turned off the vizor.

"Thieves," the woman said and began to brush her hair again.

"Criminals."

"The Society of Thieves," mused Keiris, "is about the only moral force in America Imperial. How strange! We destroy our churches and feast our souls on robbers!"

"Their victims rarely report a spiritual awakening," returned Haze-Gaunt dryly.

"Which is hardly unexpected," she retorted. "Those few who wail over their trifling losses are blind to the salvation which is brought to the many."

"No matter how the Society uses its loot, remember, it is still made up of common thieves. Simple police cases."

"Simple police cases! Just yesterday the Minister of Subversive Activities made a public statement to the effect that if they weren't obliterated within another decade—"

"I know, I know," Haze-Gaunt said impatiently, trying to cut her off.

Keiris refused to be interrupted. "—if they weren't obliterated within another decade the Thieves would destroy the present 'beneficial' balance between freeman and slave."

"He's perfectly right."

"Perhaps. But tell me this: Did my husband really found the Society of Thieves?"

"Your *ex*-husband?"

"Let's not quibble. You know who I mean."

"Yes," he agreed, "I know who you mean." For a fleeting moment his face, though completely immobile, seemed transformed into something hideous.

The man was silent for a long time. He said finally, "That's quite a story. Most of it you know as well as I."

"Perhaps I know less about it than you think. I know that you and he were bitter enemies as students at the Imperial University, that you thought he deliberately tried to excel you and defeat you in campus competitions. After graduation everyone seemed to think his researches were a shade more brilliant than yours. Somewhere along about then there was something about a duel, wasn't there?"

It had always struck Keiris a little odd that dueling had come back, complete with deadly weapons and a rigid etiquette, to a civilization so coldly scientific as the present one. Of course, it had been rationalized by many. The official attitude was one of resignation; there were laws against it, naturally, but what could the government do when the people themselves persisted in the ridiculous practice? Underneath that legal attitude, however, Keiris knew that it was secretly encouraged. She had heard many officials openly boast of their duels and explain smugly that it was instilling a healthy, vigorous spirit into the aristocracy. The age of chivalry, they maintained, had returned. Yet beneath it all, rarely voiced by anyone, was the feeling that dueling was necessary for the preservation of the state. The Society of Thieves had brought back the sword as a basic instrument for survival—the last defense of the despots.

Her question had not been answered, so she persisted, "You challenged him to a duel, didn't you? And then you disappeared for a few months."

"I fired first—and missed," said Haze-Gaunt shortly. "Muir, with his characteristic insufferable magnanimity, fired into the air. The I.P.'s were watching and we were arrested. Muir was released on probation. I was condemned and sold to a great orchard combine.

"An underground hydroponic orchard, my dear Keiris, is not the country idyll of the nineteenth century. I didn't see the sun for nearly a year. With thousands of tons of apples growing around me I was fed garbage a rat wouldn't touch. The few of my companion slaves who tried to steal fruit were detected and lashed to death. I was careful. My hatred sustained me. I could wait."

"Wait? For what?"

"Escape. We took turns, laid the plans carefully and were frequently successful. But, on the day before my turn was due, I was bought—and freed."

"How fortunate. By whom?"

"By 'a party unknown' the certificate said. But it could only have been Muir. He had been scheming, borrowing, and saving for months to fling this final gesture of contemptuous pity in my face."

The little ape-creature sensed the icy savageness in the man's voice and ran fearfully down his jacket sleeve to the back of his hand. Haze-Gaunt stroked his pet with a curled index finger.

The only sound in the room was the soft luxurious meeting of brush and black hair as Keiris continued her silent task. She marveled at the insane bitterness evoked by a simple act of humanity.

Haze-Gaunt stated, "It was not to be borne. I then decided to devote the remainder of my life to the destruction of Kennicot Muir. I could have hired an assassin, but I wanted to kill him myself. In the meantime I entered politics and advanced quickly. I knew how to use people. My year underground taught me that fear gets results.

"But even in my new career I could not escape Muir. The day I was appointed Secretary of War, Muir landed on Mercury."

"Surely," Keiris said, carefully filtering the sarcasm out of her words, "you don't accuse him of deliberately planning the coincidence?"

"What does it matter how it happened? The point is, it did happen. And such things continued to happen. A few years later, on the eve of the elections that were to make me chancellor of America Imperial, Muir returned from his trip to the sun."

"That was certainly an exciting time for the world."

"It was an exciting time for Muir, too. As if the trip alone wasn't enough to stir the populace, he announced an important discovery. He had found a way to beat the tremendous solar gravity by the continuous synthesis of solar matter into a remarkable fission fuel via an anti-grav mechanism. Again he was the toast of imperial society—and my greatest political triumph was ignored."

Keiris did not marvel at the bitterness in these words; she could too easily understand the resentment Haze-Gaunt must have felt at that time, was feeling even now. He had become a successful politician at the precise moment Muir had become a public hero. The contrast had not been flattering.

"But," he continued, his eyes narrowing, "my patience was finally rewarded. It was almost exactly ten years ago. Muir finally had the temerity to differ with me on a strictly political matter, and I knew then that I must kill him quickly or be eclipsed by him forever."

"You mean, have him—" She spoke the word without flinching. "—killed."

"No. I myself, personally, had to do it."

"Certainly not by dueling?"

"Certainly not."

"I didn't know Kim ever went in for politics," murmured Keiris.

"He didn't view it as a political question."

"What was the argument?"

"Just this: After establishing the solar stations Muir insisted that America Imperial follow his own policy in the use of muirium."

"And," Keiris continued to probe, "just what exactly was that policy?"

"He wanted production to be used to regenerate the general world standard of living and to free the slaves, whereas I, Chancellor of America Imperial, maintained that the material was needed for the defense of the Imperium. I ordered him to return to Earth and to report to me at the chancellory. We were alone in my inner office."

"Kim was unarmed, of course?"

"Of course. And when I told him that he was an enemy of the state, and that it was my duty to shoot him, he laughed."

"And so you shot him."

"Through the heart. He fell. I left the room to order his body removed. When I returned with a house-slave he—or his corpse—had vanished. Had a confederate carried him away? Had I really killed him? Who knows? Anyway the thefts began the next day."

"He was the first Thief?"

"We don't really know, of course. All we know is that all Thieves seemed invulnerable to police bullets. Was Muir wearing the same type of protective screen when I shot him? I don't suppose I'll ever know."

"Just what is the screen? Kim never discussed it with me."

"There again we don't know. The few Thieves we've taken alive don't know, either. Under Shey's persuasion they indicated that it was a velocity-response field based electrically on their individual encephalographic patterns, and was maintained by their cerebral waves. What it really does is spread the bullet impact over a wide area. It converts the momentum of the bullet into the identical momentum of a foam rubber cushion."

"But the police have actually killed screen-protected Thieves, haven't they?"

"True. We have semiportable Kades rifles that fire short-range heat beams. And then, of course, plain artillery with atomic explosive shells; the screen remains intact but the Thief dies rather quickly of internal injuries. But you're fully acquainted with the main remedy."

"The sword."

"Precisely. Since the screen resistance is proportional to the velocity of the missile, it offers no protection against the comparatively slow-moving things, such as the rapier, the hurled knife or even a club. And all this talk of rapiers reminds me that I have business with the Minister of Police before meeting Shey. You will come with me and we'll watch Thurmond at rapier practice for a few minutes."

"I didn't know your vaunted Minister of Police required practice. Isn't he the best blade in the Imperium?"

"The very best. And practice will keep him that way."

"Just one more question, Bern. As an ex-slave I should think you'd favor the abolition of slavery rather than its extension."

He replied sardonically, "Those who struggle mightily against enslavement can best savor their success by enslaving others. Read your history."

The tarsier stared fearfully at her from the shelter of Haze-Gaunt's shoulder. She could see the faces of man and beast together. There was something . . . As she studied the animal, she thought, In nightmares, I know you. You fascinate, you horrify. Yet you seem so harmless. Aloud she said, "Wait up, I'm coming."

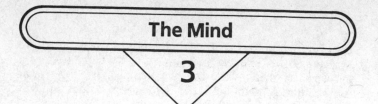

The Mind

3

An OBSEQUIOUS HOUSE-SLAVE in the red-and-gray livery of the Police Minister led them down the arched corridor to the fencing rooms. At the threshold of the chamber the slave bowed again and left them. Haze-Gaunt indicated chairs and they seated themselves unobtrusively.

Thurmond noted their arrival from the center of the gym, nodded briefly and immediately resumed a quiet conversation with his fencing opponent.

Keiris ran her eyes in grudging admiration over the Police Minister's steel-chiseled face and gorgeously muscled torso, clad lightly in a silken jacket and flowing trunks. A metallic indomitable voice floated to her.

"Do you understand the terms?"

The opponent replied thickly, "Yes, excellency." His face was covered with perspiration, and his eyes were wide and glazed.

"Remember then that if you are still alive after sixty seconds you will have your freedom. I paid nearly forty thousand unitas for you and I expect a good return for my money. Do your best."

"I shall, excellency."

Keiris turned to Haze-Gaunt sitting stiffly in the chair next to her, his arms folded across his chest. "Tell me, Bern, frankly: Doesn't it strike you that dueling nowadays is just a perverted sport? Hasn't the honor in it been lost?" She kept her voice low, away from the ears of the others.

He searched her with his hard, intelligent eyes to see if her questioning was serious. He found that it was; this was no attempt to irritate him.

"Times have changed things," he said. He decided to answer her flatly. "Yes, the traditions have been for the most part lost. The primary motivation is no longer one of 'cowardice and courage.' "

"Then it has degenerated into a mere barbaric rite."

"If it has, you can thank the Thieves for that."

"But was it ever more than that?"

"It once commanded great respect." He watched Thurmond and his opponent choosing their weapons. "Although dueling prevailed in antiquity, the modern private duel grew out of the judicial duel. In France in the sixteenth century it became very common after the famous challenge of Francis the First to his rival Charles the Fifth. After that every Frenchman seemed to think that he was called upon to use his sword in defending his honor against the slightest imputation."

"That was Europe, though," Keiris insisted, "in the old days. This is America."

Haze-Gaunt continued to watch the two men preparing for their combat. He seemed to forget the woman beside him, his reply sounding more like a recital for his own benefit. "In no part of the world was dueling so earnestly engaged in as in America. Combats were held under all sorts of conditions, with every conceivable variety of weapon. And most of them were fatal. That's what brought about laws which stamped it out until the establishment of the Imperium." He turned to look at her. "It's not remarkable that it has been revived."

"But now it has lost all moral respectability," she said. "It's just an invitation to legalized murder."

"We have laws," he replied. "No one is forced to duel."

"Like that poor fellow," said Keiris, pointing toward the center of the gym, and her black eyes flashed.

"Like him." Haze-Gaunt nodded soberly. "Now be quiet. They are ready to begin."

"*En garde!*"

Thrust, parry, feint, thrust, parry . . .

The tempo increased rapidly.

Thurmond's blade had the enchanting delicacy of an instrument that was part of its wielder. The man was incredibly light on his feet, balancing effortlessly on tiptoe—an extraordinary stance in a fencer—while his bronzed body rippled and flashed, itself a rapier, in the soft light of the chamber. His eyes were heavylidded, his face an expressionless mask. If he was breathing, Keiris could not detect it.

She transferred her study to the slave fencer and noted that the man had cast aside his despair and was defending himself with savage precision. So far his new owner had not scratched him. Perhaps in free life he really had been a dangerous duelist. Then a tiny trickle of red appeared magically on his left chest. And then one on his right chest.

Keiris held her breath and tensed her fists. Thurmond was touching each of the six sections into which a fencer's body is arbitrarily divided—a demonstration that he could kill the other at will.

The doomed man's jaw dropped, and his efforts passed from science to frenzy. When the sixth cut appeared on his lower left abdomen he screamed and sprang bodily at his tormentor.

He was dead before his disarmed blade clattered to the floor.

A gong sounded, indicating that the minute was up.

Haze-Gaunt, erstwhile pensive and silent, now arose and clapped his hands twice. "Bravo, Thurmond. Nice thrust. If you're free I'd like you to accompany me."

Thurmond handed his reddened blade to a house-slave and bowed over the corpse.

* * *

Within the transparent plastic dome the man sat trance-like. His face was partly obscured from Keiris's view by a cone-shaped metal thing that hung from the globe's ceiling and that was fitted at its lower extremity with two viewing lenses. The man was staring fixedly into the lenses.

His head was large, even for the large body that bore it. His face was a repulsive mass of red scar tissue, devoid of definable features. His hairless hands were similarly scarred and malformed.

Keiris shifted uneasily in her seat in the semicircle of spectators. On her left was Thurmond, silent, imperturbable. On her right Haze-Gaunt sat immobile in his chair, arms crossed over his chest. It was clear that he was growing impatient. Beyond him was Shey, and beyond Shey was a man she recognized as Gaines, Undersecretary for Space.

Haze-Gaunt inclined his head slightly toward Shey. "How long will this go on?" His furry pet chattered nervously, ran down his sleeve, then back to his shoulder again.

Shey, his face wreathed in perpetual smiles, raised a pudgy hand in warning. "Patience, Bern. We must await the end of the present net runs."

"Why?" asked Thurmond with mixed curiosity and indifference.

The psychologist smiled benignly. "At present the Meganet Mind is in a deep autohypnosis. To expose him to unusual exterior stimuli would rupture some of his subconscious neural networks and his usefulness to the government as an integrator of disconnected facts would be seriously impaired."

"Facts?" said Thurmond distantly. "What are these facts? Please explain."

"Of *course*," replied the rotund psychologist with amiable eagerness. "At the outset, let me say that here in this room all we have is the terminal. There's a lot you don't see: logic circuits, memory, current input, and associated hardware. All of that is located far underground, to minimize radiation damage. Memory is comprehensive, with ten to the fifteenth bytes. We access all items in all libraries: some three billion books and documents, in all languages. We have all graphics: maps of villages and galaxies. We get data from several hundred spy satellites. The Mind designed the whole thing. The logic and memory are combined into one superchip. Not really a chip, though. More of a polymeric, grapefruit-sized blob, traced out by electronmicroscope. The Mind selected the tri-di shape deliberately. It permits complete memory access in a matter of nanoseconds. The entire data output is integrated into a series of microscopic networks and fed into a viewer, to form a meganet. Each of the Mind's eyes is observing a different net projection, and each projection passes through the viewer at a speed of forty frames a second.

"One-fortieth of a second is the approximate reversal rate of the visual purple of the retina and this represents the upper limit at which the Meganet Mind can operate. His actual thought processes, of course, are much faster."

"I begin to see," murmured Haze-Gaunt, "how the Mind can read an encyclopedia within minutes but I still don't understand why he must work under autohypnosis."

Shey beamed. "One of the main traits of the human mind that distinguishes it from, for example, that of your pet is its ability to ignore trivia. When the average man sets about solving a problem he automatically excludes all that his conscious mind considers irrelevant.

"But is the rejected matter really irrelevant? Long experience tells us we can't trust our conscious mind in its rejections. That's why we say, 'Let me sleep on it.' That gives the subconscious mind an opportunity to force something to the attention of the conscious mind."

"What you're saying," said Haze-Gaunt, "is simply that the Meganet Mind is effective because he functions on a subconscious level and uses the sum total of human knowledge on every problem given him."

"Exactly!" cried the psychologist with pleasure. "How clever you are, Bern!"

"I believe the viewer is being retracted," observed Thurmond.

They waited expectantly as the man within the globe slowly sat erect and stared at them, still half-unseeing.

"Do you notice his face and hands?" burbled the psychologist. "He was burned badly in a circus fire. He used to be a mere entertainer before I discovered him. Now he's the most useful instrument in my whole collection of slaves. But look, Bern, he's going to discuss something with Gaines. Listen and judge for yourself whether you want to ask him some questions."

A transparent panel rolled aside in the dome. The Mind addressed Gaines, a tall, cavern-cheeked man.

"Yesterday," said the Mind, "you asked whether the Muir drive could be adapted for use in the *T-twenty-two*. I think it could. The conventional Muir drive depends upon the fission of muirium into americium and curium, with an energy output of four billion ergs per microgram of muirium per second.

"However, when Muir synthesized muirium from americium and curium in his first trip to the sun, he failed to realize that the element could also be synthesized from protons and energy quanta at a temperature of eighty million degrees. And the reverse is true.

"If the muirium nucleus is disrupted at eighty million degrees, the energy developed would be over forty quintillion ergs per microgram, which would be power enough to accelerate the *T-twenty-two* very quickly to a velocity beyond the speed of light, except for the theoretical limiting velocity of the speed of light."

Gaines looked dubious. "That's too much acceleration for a human cargo. Ten or eleven G's is the limit, even with a pressure-packed abdomen."

"It's an interesting question," admitted the Mind. "Like slow freezing, a few G's could be expected to rupture and destroy cell life. On the other hand, a few *million* G's administered *ab initio* with no transition from low to high acceleration, might be comparable to quick freezing in its preservation of body cells.

"However, the analogy ends there, for while freezing inhibits cell change, gravity stimulates it. Observe the effect of only one G on a plant. It causes certain of the plant cells slowly to accumulate skywards to constitute a stalk, and certain others slowly to accumulate earthward to form the rhizome structure.

"Several million G's would undoubtedly cause drastic but unpredictable micro- and macropathologic geotropic transformations. Check with the scientists working on the Geotropic Project. I can only suggest that you try various biota as passengers in the *T-twenty-two* before human beings make the trip."

"You're probably right. I'll install a Muir drive with the proper converting system at eighty million degrees."

The conversation ended perfunctorily. Gaines bowed to the group and left.

Shey turned a delighted face up to Haze-Gaunt. "Remarkable chap, this Mind, isn't he?"

"Really? I could do as well myself by mixing some old newspaper reports with a little pseudoscience and mumbo-jumbo. What can he do with something only *I* know about?" He caressed the little animal on his shoulder. "My pet here, for example?"

The Mind was not addressed directly. Yet he replied immediately in his factual monotone. "His excellency's pet appears to be a spectral tarsier."

"*Appears?* You are already lost in speculation."

"Yes, he appears to be a *tarsius spectrum*. He has the great eyes, large sensitive ears and elongated heel bone that help the tarsius in detecting insects at night and in jumping to catch them on the wing. He has the small platyrhine nose, too.

"Structurally he appears, like the spectral tarsier, higher in the evolutionary tree than the tree shrews and lemurs, lower than the monkeys, apes, and man. But appearances are deceptive. *Tarsius* is at most an arboreal quadruped. Your pet can brachiate, the same as the primates. His thumbs are opposable and he can walk erect on his hind legs for short distances."

"All that would be obvious to a keen observer," said Haze-Gaunt. "I suppose you'd say he's a mutated lemur evolving toward the primates?"

"I would not."

"No? But surely of terrestrial stock?"

"Very likely."

The chancellor relaxed and tweaked his pet's ears idly. "Then you can learn something from me." His voice was ominously cold. "This creature was recovered from the wreckage of a ship that almost certainly came from outer space. He is the living proof of an evolving biota remarkably parallel to our own." He turned languidly to Shey. "You see? He can do nothing for me. He's a fraud. You ought to have him destroyed."

"I know about the wreckage referred to," interjected the Mind quietly. "Despite its interstellar drive, as yet unknown on Earth—with the possible exception of the mechanism I just explained to Gaines for the *T-twenty-two*—there is other evidence that points to the terrestrial origin of the ship."

"What evidence?" asked Haze-Gaunt.

"Your pet. Instead of being a tarsioid reaching toward primatehood, he is more likely of human stock that has degenerated into a tarsioid line."

Haze-Gaunt said nothing. He stroked the little animal's sleek head, which peeped fearfully over his shoulder toward the Mind.

"What is the Mind talking about?" whispered Shey.

Haze-Gaunt ignored him and looked down at the Mind again. "You realize I cannot permit such inference to go unchallenged." The edge on his voice was growing sharper.

"Consider the whale and porpoise," said the Mind unhurriedly. "They seem to be as well as or better adapted to the sea than the shark. And yet we know they are not fishes but mammals, because they are warm-blooded and breathe air. From such evolutionary residua we know that their ancestors conquered dry land and later returned to the water. And it's the same with your pet. His ancestors were once human, perhaps even higher, and dwelled the earth—*because he can speak English!*"

Haze-Gaunt's lips were pressed together in a thin white line. The Mind continued relentlessly. "He talks only when the two of you are alone. Then he begs you not to go away. That's all he ever says."

Haze-Gaunt addressed Keiris without turning his head. "Have you eavesdropped?"

"No," she lied.

"Perhaps you do have some extraordinary power of factual synthesis," Haze-Gaunt said to the Mind. "Suppose, then, you tell me why the little beast keeps begging me not to 'go away' when I have no intention of leaving the Imperium?"

"He can foresee the future to that extent," stated the Mind tonelessly.

Haze-Gaunt gave no sign of either believing or disbelieving. He rubbed his lower lip with his thumb and regarded the Mind thoughtfully. "I am not ignoring the possibility that you may be a fraud. Still, there is a question that has been troubling me for some time. On the answer to this question my future—even my life—may depend. Can you tell me both the question and its answer?"

"Oh, come now, Bern," interrupted Shey. "After all—"

He was interrupted in turn. "The Imperial American government," intoned the Mind, "would like to launch a surprise attack on the Eastern Federation within six weeks. The chancellor wishes to know whether factors unknown to him will require the postponement of the attack."

Haze-Gaunt was leaning forward in his chair, body tense. Shey was not smiling.

"That's the question," admitted the chancellor. "What is the answer?"

"Factors that may require postponement of the attack do in fact exist."

"Indeed? What are they?"

"One of them I do not know. The answer depends on data presently unavailable."

"I'll get the data," said Haze-Gaunt with growing interest. "What's necessary?"

"A competent analysis of a section of a certain star chart. Four years ago the Lunar Station began sending me microfilm plates of both celestial hemispheres by the square second. One of these plates is of particular interest, and I feel that what it shows may have a bearing on the future of civilization. It should be analyzed immediately."

"What sort of bearing?" demanded Haze-Gaunt.

"I don't know."

"Eh? Why not?"

"His conscious mind can't fathom his subconscious," explained Shey, fingering his rich robes. "All his conscious mind can do is bring to light the impressions of his subconscious mind."

"Very well. I'll put the lunar staff to work on it."

"A routine examination will prove worthless," warned the Mind. "I could recommend only two or three astrophysicists in the system capable of the necessary analysis."

"Name one."

"Ames has recently been attached to the staff of Undersecretary Gaines. Perhaps Gaines could be persuaded to lend—"

"He'll do it," said Haze-Gaunt succinctly. "Now, you mentioned 'factors'—in the plural. I presume the star plate isn't the only one."

"There is another factor of uncertainty," said the Mind. "It involves the personal safety of the chancellor as well as the ministers and consequently bears on the question of postponing the attack."

Haze-Gaunt looked sharply at the man in the globe. The Mind returned the stare with emerald-basilisk eyes. The chancellor coughed. "This other factor—"

The Mind resumed placidly, "The most powerful creature—I hesitate to call him a man—on Earth today is neither Lord Chancellor Haze-Gaunt nor the Dictator of the Eastern Federation."

"Don't tell us it's Kennicot Muir," said Haze-Gaunt sardonically.

"The creature I have in mind is a professor at the Imperial University named Alar—possibly so named because of his winged mind. He is very likely a Thief, but that's of minor consequence."

At the word "Thief," Thurmond looked interested. "Why is he dangerous? Thieves are limited to defense by their code."

"Alar seems to be a mutant with potentially great physical and mental powers. If he ever discovers he has these powers, considering his present political viewpoint, no human being on earth would be safe from him, code or no code."

"Just what are his potentialities?" queried Shey. "Is he a hypnotist? A telekineticist?"

"I don't know," admitted the Mind. "I can only offer my opinion that he is dangerous. *Why* is another matter."

Haze-Gaunt appeared lost in thought. Finally, without looking up, he said, "Thurmond, will you and Shey be in my office in one hour? Bring Eldridge of the War Office with you. Keiris, you will return to your rooms in the company of your bodyguard. It will take you all evening to dress for the Imperatrix's ball tonight."

A few minutes later the four left the room. Keiris, taking a last look backward, met the enigmatic, unblinking eyes of the Mind and was troubled. He had been telling her at various intervals during the interview, by the code they had worked out long before, that she must be prepared to receive a Thief in her rooms tonight and protect him from his pursuers.

And Haze-Gaunt would be expecting her at the masked ball simultaneously.

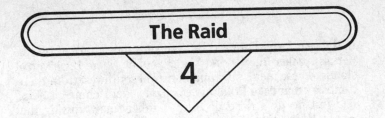

The Raid

4

FROM HIS SEAT at the grand piano Alar peered over the music sheets toward his two friends, Micah Corrips, Professor of Ethnology, and John Haven, Professor of Biology, who were huddled in complete absorption over their voluminous manuscript.

Alar's dark, oversized eyes glanced at the two savants briefly; then his gaze went past them, by the disordered stacks of books and papers, beyond the mounted row of human and semi-human skeletons, past the urn of coffee gradually boiling dry near the street window and out over the university campus, where a large black truck was pulling up quietly in the late afternoon behind a hedge of Grecian junipers. It simply stopped. Nobody got out.

His pulse was climbing slowly. He sounded a certain chord on the piano keyboard. Two men heard him, he knew, but did not seem alarmed.

"Now, Micah, read what you have there," said Haven to the ethnologist.

Corrips, a large vigorous man with friendly blue eyes and a classroom manner so seductive that the great university auditorium had been assigned to him as a lecture room, picked up the preface and began to read.

" 'We may imagine, if we like, that early one afternoon

in the year forty thousand B.C. the advance group of Neandertals reached the Rhone Valley, about where Lyons now stands. These men and women, driven southwest from their hunting grounds in Bohemia by slowly encroaching glaciers, had lost nearly a third of their number since crossing the frozen Rhine the previous January. There were no longer any children or very aged people in the group.

" 'These men from eastern Europe were not handsome. They were squat, massive, almost neckless, with beetling brow ridges and flattened nostrils. They walked with bent knees, on the outer edges of their feet, as do the higher anthropoids.

" 'Even so, they were tremendously more civilized than the brutish Eoanthropus (Heidelberg man?) into whose territory they were marching. Eoanthropus's sole tool was a crude piece of flint, chipped and shaped to fit his hand, which he used to grub at roots and occasionally to strike at reindeer from ambush.

" 'He passed his short dim-witted life in the open. Neanderthal, on the contrary, made flint spearheads, knives and saws. For these he used large flintflakes rather than the core of the flint. He lived in caves and cooked over a fire. He must have had some idea of a spirit world and a life in the hereafter, for he buried his dead with weapons and artifacts. The group leader—' "

"Excuse me, gentlemen," Alar broke in quietly. "I register one fifty-five." His fingers continued to ripple on through the second movement of the "Pathétique." He had not taken his eyes from the music sheets since he had first looked across the room and through the window in response to the warning acceleration of his strange heart.

" 'The leader,' " continued Corrips, " 'gray, grizzled, ruthless—paused and sniffed the air moving up the valley. He smelled reindeer blood a few hundred yards down the draw, also another, unknown smell, like yet unlike the noisome blend of grime, sweat and dung that characterized his own band.' "

Haven arose, tapped his pipe gently on the ash tray lying on the big table, stretched his small, wiry frame with tigerish languor and walked slowly toward the coffee urn by the window.

Alar was now well into the final movement of the "Pathétique." He watched Haven carefully.

Corrips droned on resonantly without the faintest change of inflection, but Alar knew the ethnologist was watching his collaborator from the corner of his eye.

" 'The old man turned to the little band and shook his flint-tipped spear to show that the spoor had been struck. The other men held their spears up, signifying that they understood and would follow silently. The women faded into the sparse shrubbery of the valley slope.

" 'The men followed the reindeer path on down the gully and within a few minutes peered through a thicket at an old male Eoanthropus, three females of assorted ages and two children, all lying curled stuporously under a windfall of branches and debris that overhung the gully bank. Blood still drained sluggishly from a half-devoured reindeer carcass lying under the old man's head.' "

Alar followed Haven with narrowed eyes. The little biologist poured a cup of coffee of the consistency of mud, added a little cream from the portofrij and stirred it absently, the while looking out of the window from the shadows of the room.

" 'Some sixth sense warned Eoanthropus of danger. The old male shook his five-hundred-pound body and convulsed into a snarling squat over the reindeer, searching through nearsighted eyes for the rash interlopers. He feared nothing but the giant cave bear, *Ursus spelaeus*. The females and children scurried behind him with mingled fear and curiosity.

" 'Through the green foliage the invaders stared thunderstruck. It was immediately evident to them that the killers were some sort of animal, pretending to be men. The more intelligent of the Neandertals, including the old leader, exchanged glances of wrathful indignation. Without more ado the leader broke through the brush and raised his spear high with an angry shout.

" 'He was seized by the conviction that these offensive creatures were strange, hence intolerable, that the sooner they were killed the more comfortable he would feel. He drew back his heavy spear and hurled it with all his strength. It passed through the heart of Eoanthropus to protrude half a foot beyond the back.' "

Haven was frowning when he turned away from the window. He lifted the cup of coffee to his mouth and, just before he drank, his lips silently formed the words, "Audio search beam."

Alar knew that Corrips had caught the signal, even though the latter continued to read as though nothing had happened.

" 'The brute-mind behind that hurtling spear, faced with the problem of an alien people, arrived at a solution by a simple thalamic response, uncomplicated by censorship of the frontal lobes—kill first, examine later.

" 'This instinctive reaction, a vestige perhaps from the minuscule mental organization of his insectivore ancestor (Zalambdolestes?), dating probably back to the Cretaceous, has characterized every species of Hominidae before and since Neandertal.

" 'The reaction is still strong, as two World Wars bear horrible witness. If the man with the spear could have reasoned first and hurled second, his descendants might have reached the stars within a very few millennia.

" 'And now that fissionable materials are being mined directly from the sun's surface in enormous quantities by America Imperial, the Western and Eastern hemispheres will not long delay another attempt to contest the superiority of their respective cultures. This time, however, neither side can hope for victory, stalemate, or even defeat.

" 'The war will end, simply because there will be no human beings left to fight—if we except a hundred or so anımal-like creatures huddling in the farthest corridors of the underground cities, licking their radiation sores and sharing with a few rats the corpses that lie so well-preserved everywhere (there being no putrefying bacteria remaining to decompose the dead). But even the ghouls are sterile and in another decade—' "

There was a knock at the door.

Haven and Corrips exchanged quick glances. Then Haven put down his coffee and walked toward the foyer. Corrips looked quickly about the room, reaffirming the positions of their sabers, which hung with innocent decorativeness from straps among the Hominidae skeletons.

They heard Haven's voice from the hallway. "Good evening, sir—? Why, it's General Thurmond. What a delightful surprise, general! I recognized you at once but of course you don't know me. I'm Professor Haven."

"Mind if I come in, Dr. Haven?" There was something chilling and deadly in that dry voice.

"Not at all! Why, bless my soul we're honored. Come in! Micah! Alar! It's General Thurmond, Minister of Police!"

Alar knew that the man's effusiveness covered unusual nervousness.

Corrips timed his approach so that the group would coalesce about the Hominidae. Alar, following close behind, observed uneasily that the ethnologist's hands were twitching. Were they so afraid of just one man? His respect for Thurmond was increasing rapidly.

Except for a piercing appraisal of Alar, Thurmond ignored the introductions. "Professor Corrips," he rasped gently, "you were reading something very peculiar just before I knocked. You know, of course, that we had a search beam on the study?"

"Did you? How odd. I was reading from a book that Dr. Haven and I are writing—*Suicide of the Human Race*. Were you interested?"

"Only incidentally. It's really a matter for the Minister

of Subversive Activities. I shall report it, of course, for whatever action he deems best. But I'm really here on another matter."

Alar sensed the tension mount by a full octave. Corrips was breathing loudly—Haven, apparently, not at all. Thurmond's feral eyes, he knew, had not missed the cluster of sabers dangling with the Hominidae.

"What," asked the officer abruptly, "is the Geotropic Project?"

"Surely not a question of subversion, general?" said Corrips. "We understand the project was recommended by the Meganet Mind himself."

"Irrelevant," said the visitor calmly. "Please summarize it briefly."

The two professors exchanged glances. Corrips shrugged. "The project investigates the effects of high velocities and accelerations on living organisms. In the general case we used an extremely fast centrifuge, providing a gravity gradient developing from one G to several million over a period of weeks."

"Results?" said Thurmond.

"Results varied. And are still not understood."

"Examples?" said the visitor.

"Well, in one case obelia, a sea-dwelling primitive polyp-feeder, evolved forward into the sea anemone. On the other hand, radiolaria, a silica-secreting protozoa, evolved backward to limax amoeba—which doesn't secrete anything. In another case, euglena, the first of the one-celled protozoa to possess chlorophyll, as well as being the first plant-like form, fell back down the evolutionary ladder to become a simple flagellate."

"Higher forms?" asked Thurmond.

"Various," said Corrips. He did not elaborate.

The general lifted his hand indolently, as though to indicate it didn't matter. "I understand that the project is staffed largely with persons with—impediments," he said coldly.

"Yes," said Corrips. The word faded into a whisper.

"They work for you?"

"We direct and assist them in their work," explained Haven.

"You control them," said Thurmond flatly.

No one answered. Haven wiped perspiring hands on the sides of his coat.

"May I see the personnel register?" asked Thurmond.

The two professors hesitated. Then Corrips stepped to the desk and returned with a black book. He gave it to Thurmond, who leafed through it idly, examining two or three of the photographs with gloomy curiosity. "This chap with no legs," he said. "What does he do within the project?"

Alar's pulse beat had climbed to one hundred seventy a minute.

Corrips cleared his throat. "The Gemini ..." The words were garbled. He coughed and tried again. "The Gemini Run."

Thurmond looked at him with thinly veiled amusement. "Which is?"

"Two tree shrew fetuses in the centrifuge. Extraordinary gravities, recorded under strobe lights at picoseconds. One went up the scale, to become the fetus of what looked like a lemur. The other retrogressed to a lizard-like form. Just before it died it looked rather like a dog fish."

"He can't carry a gun, can he?"

"Who? Oh, the Gemini scientist?"

Alar watched the six black-shirted I.P.'s ease quietly into the room behind Thurmond.

"Of course not," snapped Corrips. "His contributions lie in an altogether different—"

"Then the government can't be expected to continue his support," interjected Thurmond. He ripped the sheet from the book and handed it to the officer who stood just behind him. "And here's another," he said, frowning at the next page. "A blind woman. No use at all in a factory, is she?"

"Her mother," said Haven tightly, "collaborated with

Kennicot Muir in determining the Nine Fundamental Equations that culminated in the establishment of our solarions on the surface of the sun. This child, in her own right, is one of the most brilliant minds in the Geotropic Project. For instance, she has fed all our data into the computer, and she has put the question, 'What would be the effect on a human being?'"

"The answer?"

Haven clenched his fists. "I—we—we need more work."

"But what does it look like so far? What effect on human beings?"

The professor sighed. "It would be a bit like the Gemini Run. According to the computer, two samples of the same species would have to be associated together to show the effect. In the hypothetical case, one would *evolve*, the other would *devolve*."

"And this girl programmed the computer for *that*?"

"Yes."

"Most unscientific, Professor Haven. In fact, it's downright ridiculous." Thurmond studied the registry sheet. "If that's the best this girl can do, you'll never miss her. More to the point, she's incapable of precision labor and her mother was an associate of Muir, a known traitor." He ripped the sheet out and passed it back to a young officer.

"Just what does the lieutenant intend doing with those sheets?" asked Haven with a rising voice. He moved his hand carelessly to the clavicle of the Cro-Magnon skeleton, a few inches from the sabers.

"We're going to take all your research staff away, professor."

Haven's mouth opened and closed. He seemed to shrink where he stood. Finally he said hesitantly: "For what reason, sir?"

"For the reason I have said. They are useless to the Imperium."

"Not really sir," Haven said slowly. "Their usefulness must be evaluated in terms of the long range good they will do for humanity—and, of course, the Imperium. . . ."

"Perhaps," Thurmond said unemotionally. "But we shall not take that chance."

"Then," Haven asked cautiously, "then you plan to . . . ?"

"Do you insist that I be precise?"

"Yes."

"They will be sold to the highest bidder—probably a charnel-house."

Alar found himself licking pallid lips. It could not be happening but it was happening. Twenty-two young men and women, some of the most brilliant minds in the Imperium, were going to be snuffed out with casual brutality—*why*?

Corrips's voice was hardly a whisper. "What do you want?"

"Alar," stated Thurmond icily. "Give me Alar and keep the others."

"No!" cried Haven, staring white-faced at Thurmond. He turned to Corrips and found confirmation there.

Alar listened to his voice. It seemed that of another man. "I must go with you, of course," he said to Thurmond.

Haven shot out a restraining hand. "No, boy! You haven't the faintest idea what it's all about. You're worth far more than any two dozen minds on Earth. If you love humanity do as we tell you!"

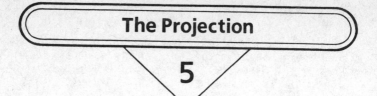

The Projection

5

THURMOND CALLED A quiet command over his shoulders. "Shoot them."

Six blasts of lead, urged by the titanic pressures of fission-generated steam, bounced harmlessly off the three men and ricocheted about the walls.

The sabers were no longer hanging from the Hominidae.

And Thurmond's blade was lunging for Alar's heart.

Only the tightest breast parry saved the Thief. The lieutenant and his men, evidently hand picked, were forcing the two older men back down the wall.

"Alar!" cried Haven. "Don't fight Thurmond! The trapdoor! We'll cover you!"

The Thief flung an anguished look toward the professors. Haven broke free from the wall and joined Alar, who was as yet miraculously unbloodied. They immediately crashed into the wing of the grand piano.

The floor dropped from under them.

Alar's last view of the study was Corrips's body at the foot of the wall with his face cut away. With a shriek of grief he flung his sword futilely at Thurmond, and then the trap wings closed over his head.

As he careened through the tunnel his nostrils were assailed by the musty, mysterious smell of earth. His face broke spider webs. The little eight-leggers must live on smaller, blundering insects, he thought. He and Haven dashed by algae growing in vague green circles around the dim intermittent lights. A couple of tiny winged insects flew off in alarm. A diminutive underground ecosystem. Predators and prey. He deeply sympathized. Like rabbits, he and his friend were fleeing through the emergency exit burrow. The wolves behind them would break down the entrance trapdoor in another sixty seconds. Time enough. Unless more wolves awaited them at the exit. Keep running. No choice. Not now. Too late for anything else. Far too late. He could have—*should* have—saved Corrips.

In the semi-darkness he accosted Haven bitterly. "Why didn't you let me go with Thurmond?"

"Do you think it was easy for Micah and me, boy?" panted the professor brokenly. "You'll understand some day. Right now we've got to get you to a safer place."

"But what about Micah?" insisted Alar.

"He's dead. We can't even bury him. Come along, now."

They hurried silently to the end of the tunnel, half a mile away, where it opened into a dead-end alley from behind a mass of debris.

"The nearest Thief rendezvous is six blocks up the street. You know the one?"

Alar nodded dumbly.

"I can't run as fast as you," continued Haven. "You've got to make it alone. You simply must. No questions. Off with you, now."

The Thief touched the older man's bloody sleeve silently, then turned and ran.

He ran swiftly in the center of the streets, easily, rhythmically, breathing through dilated nostrils. Everywhere were the thin, weary faces of free laborers and clerks returning from the day's work. Peddlers and beggars, dressed in drab cast-off garments but not yet slaves, dotted the sidewalks.

Three hundred meters above him twelve or fifteen

armed helicopters followed leisurely. He sensed that a three-dimensional net was closing in on him. Road blocks were probably being set up ahead as well as on the side streets.

He had two squares to go.

A trio of searchlights stabbed down at him from the darkening skies like an audible chord of doom. To attempt to dodge the beams was futile. Still, explosive shells would follow within seconds and a near hit could kill him.

Subconsciously he noted that the streets had suddenly become empty. When Thief-hunting, the I.P.'s fired their artillery with fine disregard of careless street dwellers. He would never make the Thief underground station. He must hide now or never.

With flashing eyes he looked about him, and found what he wanted, an entrance to the slave underworld. It was fifty yards away, and he sprinted toward it frantically.

Above him, he knew, some thirty narrowed eyes were squinting into gun sights, trigger fingers with cool, unhurried efficiency were squeezing. . . .

He flung himself into the gutter.

The shell struck ten feet in front of him. He was up instantly, coughing and stunned, but invisible in the swirling dust clouds. Pieces of brick and cobblestone were falling all about him. Two of the spotlights were roving nervously over the edge of the cloud nearest the underworld entrance. The other was playing rapidly and erratically around the periphery of the cloud. He couldn't even make the slave entrance. He waited for the spotlight to pass, then dashed for the nearest tenement door.

The door was boarded and locked. He pounded frantically.

For the first time he felt—hunted. And with that cornered feeling time slowed down and finally crept. He knew that his senses had simply accelerated. He noted several things. His ears caught the heavy grinding of an armored car churning around the corner on two wheels, with headlights that swept the entire street.

He saw that the dust had settled and that two of the 'copter searchlights were combing the area methodically. A third beam had settled motionless on the underground stairway entrance. That beam was the only real obstacle. It was a neat problem in stimulus-response physiology. Stimulus—observer sees object enter white circular field ten feet in diameter. Response—pull trigger before object leaves field.

Like a frightened deer he leaped between the two converging beams of the armored car and sped toward the brilliantly lighted stairs. He was struck twice by small-arm fire from the car but his armor absorbed it easily. The turret computer would need only milliseconds to train the gun on him. But that was all the time he needed.

He was in the lighted area of the stairs now, hurtling downward toward the first landing. He had tried desperately to clear all the steps, and he did. He crashed to the concrete platform and immediately stretched out flat as a shell shattered the entrance.

He was up again instantly, tearing down the remaining flights to the first underground level of the slave city. It would take his pursuers a few seconds to pick their way through that wreck of muck and rubble. He would need the delay.

He eased out of the stairway cautiously, leaned against the wall and peered about him, sucking in the foul air gratefully. On this level lived the higherclass slaves, those who had sold themselves into bondage for twenty years or less.

It was time for the night shifts to be leaving the slave compounds, accompanied by bullet-browed squad masters. They would be transported to the fields, mines, mills or wherever the slave contractor ordered them sent. There they would work out the nameless fraction of their lives that they had sold.

By crossing through these grim work parties he should be able to make his way to the ascending stairs *behind* the armored car and resume his flight to the Thief hideaway.

But not a person was moving in the silent substreets.

The row on row of slave compounds, up and down the narrow streets, were shut up tightly. That could not have been done within a few minutes. It bespoke hours of preparation by Thurmond. It must be that way on every level, even to Hell's Row, where diseased and manacled wretches labored in eternal gloom. He whirled in alarm. An armored car was rolling through the darkened street toward him.

He understood then that most of the small mobile artillery available to Thurmond from his own police forces, as well as a considerable contingent borrowed from Eldridge of the War Department, had been placed strategically on all slave levels, hours before, just to kill him.

They had driven him underground to finish him.

But why? Why was it so important to kill him? Not because he was a Thief. The government harbored a vengeful bitterness against Thieves, but this was a turnout of force on a scale for suppressing revolution.

What gigantic danger did he represent to Haze-Gaunt?

Haven and Corrips must have known more about him than they had ever admitted. If by some remote chance he ever saw Haven again, he would certainly have some questions to ask him.

Down the street to the left another armored car was rumbling up. Almost simultaneously searchlights shot from both cars, blinding him. He dropped to the ground and buried his face in the crook of his arm. The two shells exploded on the steel wall behind him and the concussion threw him into the center of the street between the oncoming cars.

His coat was ripped to shreds and his nose was bleeding. His head was spinning a bit, but otherwise he was undamaged. For the moment he decided to lie where he had fallen.

One of the spotlights was playing over the dust cloud. Alar watched the beam glowing above him like the sun attempting to burn its rays through an overcast sky. As the dust began to settle the light, too, was dropping closer to him. He knew that it was marking time, waiting to reveal a corpse—his corpse. The other spotlight was darting nearly everywhere along the street where he lay. They were taking no chances that the shot had not been fatal.

Alar examined the ground around him. There was some rubble now, covering the rough macadam-topped cobble-stones, and a layer of dust, but there were no holes to slide into, no depressions or objects large enough to hide behind. The street was open around him, with the distant cars and buildings boxing him in. He estimated his chances of escape by springing erect, and saw immediately that he had none. He could only crouch there and hope. Hope for what? In a few seconds the accusing finger of light must point at him and the grim game would continue.

It would not be a long game.

As he lay there in the foul humid dirt, he wished fervently that he had the legendary lives of the cat, and that one of them would emerge from the luminous cloud of dust. He could see himself staggering through the settling fog surrendering one life after another to the firing guns. Buying enough time to—

What was that?

He blinked and stared. He *was* seeing a figure. A man with a tattered coat very much like his own stumbled through the haze. *Who?* It didn't matter—in seconds the figure would be struck down, blasted into lifelessness. But the man was conscious of the danger. He looked up the street both ways, noting the armored cars, now very near, then began to run quickly along the steel wall that paralleled the street from the entrance stairway.

While Alar stared, thunderstruck, the farthest car, now about abreast of the stranger, fired point blank. At the same time the other pursuing car passed within a few inches of the Thief and sped on to the chase.

Now if the stranger emerged unscathed from the sure hit . . . ! And he did! Hugging the wall, the shadowy form continued to run up the street.

Two more explosions came, very close together.

Even before he heard them, Alar was running down the dark street in the opposite direction.

Within forty seconds, if he were lucky, he would reach the stair formerly guarded by the first car and would be "upstairs" again. There he would have time to wonder about the man who, perhaps unwittingly, had saved his life.

Had some fool blundered through the police blockade at the head of the stairs into the blossoming shell dust? He rejected that immediately, not only because he trusted the I.P.'s to maintain a leakproof watch over the entrance above, but also because he had recognized the face.

Yes, he had finally recognized the face when the lights had blazed squarely upon it. He had seen it many times before: the slightly bulging brow, the large dark eyes, the almost girlish lips—yes, he knew that face well.

It was his own.

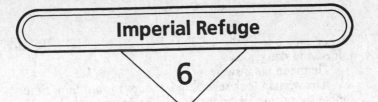

A N HOUR LATER Alar—poised statue-like on the marble sill, balancing on one knee with steel fingertips extended to the cold stone surface—*stared*.

The woman was about his own age, dressed in a white evening gown of remarkable softness and luster. Her long blue-black hair, interlaced with inconspicuous gold netting, was gathered in a wide band over her left breast.

Her head seemed unusually large, rather like his own, with large black eyes that studied him carefully. The expertly rouged lips were in odd contrast to the pale, utterly expressionless cheeks. She was not standing straight, but with her left hip slightly dipping, so that the left thigh and knee were sharply defined beneath her gown.

The whole impression was one of alert hauteur.

Alar was conscious of a growing, indefinable elation.

He slipped noiselessly down to the floor and moved to the side of the window, where he was invisible from the courtyard, and turned to face her again—just as something flashed by his face and buried itself in the wall paneling at his ear.

He froze.

"I am glad you are logical," she replied quietly. "It saves time. Are you the fugitive Thief?" He saw the flashes

49

in her eyes and evaluated her character quickly: self-contained and dangerous.

He made no answer.

The woman took several quick steps toward him, simultaneously raising her right arm. The movement drew the white gown across the front of her figure and emphasized her curves. In her upraised hand was a second knife. It gleamed wickedly in the soft light.

"It will be to your advantage to answer truthfully and quickly," she said.

He still made no answer. His eyes were opened wide now and boring into hers, but those large eyes with their black fire within were steady, unflinching.

A short laugh burst unexpectedly from her lips. "Do you think you can stare me down?" she asked. The knife waggled suggestively above her fingers. "Come, now. If you are the Thief, produce your mask."

He gave an ironic grin, shrugged his shoulders and pulled out the mask.

"Why didn't you go to your Thief rendezvous? Why did you come here?" She lowered her arm, but kept the knife firmly in her hand.

He peered at her narrowly. "I tried. All paths were blocked for miles. The weakest protection led here, to the chancellory. Who are you?"

Keiris ignored the question. She moved a step nearer him, scrutinizing him from his soft shoes to his black skull cap. Then she scanned his face and a faint, slightly puzzled frown gathered between her eyebrows.

"Have you seen me before?" he asked. There was something in her expression which bothered him. It added mysteriously to the elation building within him.

She ignored that question, too. She said, "What shall I do with you?" The query was solemn, demanding a serious answer.

He almost said, facetiously, "Call the I.P.'s, they'll know what to do." Instead he said simply, "Help me."

"I must leave," she mused. "Yet I can't desert you. These rooms will be searched before the hour is out."

"Then you will help?" He immediately felt stupid for his words. Usually he met the unexpected in complete possession of himself—it disturbed him to find that this woman could disturb him. To recover his balance, he added quickly, "Perhaps I can leave with you?"

"I have to put in an appearance at the ball," she explained.

"Ball?" The Thief considered the possibilities rapidly, accepting her help now as a matter of fact. "Why can't I come along? I'll even escort you."

She studied him curiously. Her rouged lips had parted just enough for him to see the whiteness of her teeth. "This is a masked ball."

"Like this?" He pulled on the Thief mask coolly.

Her eyes widened imperceptibly. "I accept your invitation."

If he had not, one short hour ago, lost all sense of probability and proportion, he might have toyed briefly with such words as fantastic, preposterous and insane, and wondered when the whistle of the coffee urn would awaken him.

He bowed ironically. "It is my pleasure."

She continued without humor, "You intend, of course, to leave the festival rooms at the first opportunity. Let me assure you that it would be very dangerous. You are known to be in this vicinity, and the palace grounds are swarming with police."

"So?"

"Wander through the ballroom and assembly room for a while and then we'll try to arrange your escape."

"We?" he asked with mock suspicion.

She smiled at this, with just the slightest twist at one corner of her mouth to make it particularly provocative to him. "The Society, of course. Who else?" She glanced down to place the knife on a small end table. Her lashes, he noticed, were long and black, like her hair, and emphasized

the unusual paleness of her cheeks. He found he had to
exert himself to concentrate on her words. Was she teasing
him?

"So! You're the beautiful Thief spy within the palace
walls!" His own mouth was mirroring her smile.

"Not at all." She was suddenly cautious and her smile
flickered away. "Will you do as I say?"

He had no choice and nodded his head. "Tell me this,"
he said. "What do the newscasters say about the affair at the
Geotropic Project?"

She hesitated for the first time, but seemed to lose none
of her poise. "Dr. Haven escaped."

He sucked in his breath. "And the staff?"

"Sold."

He leaned wearily against the wall, and gradually became conscious of sweat dripping in irritating rivulets down
his legs. His armpits were soaking, his face and forearms
were stinging with an odorous melange of perspiration and
grime.

"I'm sorry, Thief."

He looked at her and saw that she meant it. "It's over,
then," he said heavily, walking to her vanity dresser and
peering into the mirror. "I shall need a shower and depilatory. And some clothes. Can you find some for me? And
don't forget a saber."

"I can provide everything. You'll find the bathroom
over there."

Fifteen minutes later she took his right arm and they
walked sedately down the hall toward the broad stairs that
coiled in one beautiful sweep to the great reception chamber. Alar fussed nervously with his mask and eyed the magnificent tapestries and paintings that lined the cold marble
walls.

Everything was in exquisite taste, but he got the impression that it was the hired taste of a decorating firm—that
the people who passed their brilliant, insecure days in these
rooms had long ago lost their ability to appreciate the subtle

sunlight of Renoir or the cataclysmic color-bursts of Van Gogh.

"Leave your mask alone," whispered his companion. "You look fine."

They were descending the stairs now. He couldn't seize the whole picture—just isolated scraps. This was existence on a scale he had never expected to experience. Solid gold stair handrail. Carpets with pile that seemed to come up to his ankles. Intricately sculptured Carrara balusters. Luminous alabaster lighting everywhere. The vista of the reception chamber rushing up to them. A thousand unknown men and women.

It was all strange, but he felt that he had known it all forever, that he belonged here.

From time to time the brightly uniformed reception master announced the names of late-comers through the public address microphone. Here and there, among the sea of heads, were eyes staring up at him and the woman.

And suddenly they were at the foot of the stairs, and the reception master was bowing deeply and saying:

"Good evening, madame."

"Good evening, Jules."

Jules eyed Alar with apologetic curiosity. "I'm afraid, excellency—"

The Thief muttered coldly, "Dr. Hallmarck."

Jules bowed again. "Of course, sir." He picked up the microphone and called smoothly: "Dr. Hallmarck, escorting Madame Haze-Gaunt!"

Keiris ignored the shocked look the Thief threw at her. "You don't have to wear your mask all the time," she suggested. "Just when you see someone looking suspicious. Come along; I'll introduce you to a group of men. Work yourself into an argument and no one will pay any attention to you. I'm going to leave you with Senator Donnan. He's loud, but harmless."

Senator Donnan threw back his barrel chest impressively. "I run a free press, Dr. Hallmarck," he said to Alar. "I say what I want to. I print what I want to. I think even

Haze-Gaunt would be afraid to close me down. I get on people's nerves. They read me whether they want to or not."

Alar looked at him curiously. The stories he had heard of the Senator had not left an impression of a Champion of the Downtrodden. "Indeed?" he said politely.

The Senator continued. "I say, treat the slaves as though they were once human beings, just like ourselves. They've got rights, you know. Treat 'em poorly, and they'll die on you. The slaves in my printing shops used to complain of the noise. I gave them relief."

"I heard about that once, Senator. Very humane. Removed their eardrums, didn't you?"

"Right. No more complaints, now, about *anything*. Hah! There's old Perkins, the international banker. Hiya, Perk! Meet Professor Hallmarck."

Alar bowed, Perkins nodded sourly.

Donnan laughed. "I killed his Uniform Slave Act in the Senate Slave Committee. Old Perk is unrealistic."

"Most of us thought your proposed Slave Act rather striking, Mr. Perkins," said Alar suavely. "The provision for the condemnation and sale of debtors particularly interested me."

"A sound clause, sir. It would clear the streets of loafers."

Donnan chuckled. "I'll say it would. Perk controls eighty percent of the credit in the Imperium. Let a poor devil get a couple of unitas behind in his installment payment and *bang*—Perk has himself a slave worth several thousand unitas, for almost nothing."

The financier's mouth tightened. "Your statement, Senator, is exaggerated. Why the legal fees alone . . ." He moved away mumbling.

Donnan seemed vastly amused. "All kinds here tonight, professor. Ah, here comes something interesting. The Imperatrix, Juana-Maria, in her motorchair with Shimatsu, the Eastern Fed Ambassador, and Talbot, the Toynbeean Historian, on either side of her."

Alar watched the approaching trio with great interest. Her Imperial Majesty ... impossible, yet inevitable, given all the circumstances.

During the previous century, fear had jelled the loose system of hemispheric treaties, mutual defense pacts, and alliances into a cumbersome confederacy. A subsequent series of emergencies (including a devastating misfire in a silo near Moscow) had buried ancient mistrusts under strata of threatened holocaust, and so the final irrevocable step had been taken: during this period, called The Crises, all countries of the Western Hemisphere had united under the hegemony of what had once been the United States of America. The Latins had proposed a figurehead imperial family for the new superstate. Imperial America? At first, Washington had laughed. On the other hand, why not? Rich, powerful families, enduring as any Egyptian dynasty, authenticated by periodic assassinations, had long controlled the United States. It but remained to formally ennoble them.

Alar joined the group in a deep bow as the trio drew near and regarded the titular ruler of the Western Hemisphere curiously. The Imperatrix was an old woman, small and twisted in body, but her eyes sparkled and her face was mobile and attractive, despite its burden of wrinkles.

It was rumored that Haze-Gaunt had caused the bomb to be planted in the Imperial carriage that had taken the lives of the Imperator and his three sons. That bomb had also left the Imperatrix bedridden for years and consequently incapable of vetoing his chancellorship. By the time she had been able to get about in a motorchair, the reins of the Imperium had passed completely from the House of Chatham-Perez into the hardened palms of Bern Haze-Gaunt.

"Gentlemen, good evening," said Juana-Maria. "We're in luck tonight."

"We're always lucky to have you around, ma'am," said Donnan with genuine respect.

"Oh, don't be idiotic, Herbert. A very important and dangerous Thief, a Professor Alar at the University—can you imagine?—escaped a strong police trap and has been traced to the palace grounds. He may be in the palace at this very moment.

"General Thurmond is seething in his quiet way, and he's thrown up a perfectly tremendous guard around the grounds and is having the whole palace searched. He is taking personal charge of our protection. Isn't it thrilling?" Her voice seemed dry and mocking.

"Glad to hear it," commented Donnan with sincerity. "The rascals looted my personal safe only last week. Had to free forty men to get the stuff back. It's high time they caught the ringleaders."

Alar swallowed uncomfortably behind his mask and looked about him covertly. There was no sign of Thurmond yet, but several men that his trained eye identified as plainclothes I.P.'s were filtering slowly and attentively through the assembly. One of them, several yards away, was studying him quietly. Finally he passed on.

"Why don't you yourself do something about the Thieves, your majesty?" demanded Donnan. "They're ruining your Imperium."

Juana-Maria smiled. "Are they really? But what if they are?—which I doubt! Why should I do anything about it? I do what pleases me. My father was a politician and a soldier. It pleased him to fuse the two Americas into one during the Crises. If our civilization survives a few hundred years longer, he will undoubtedly be accorded his place as a maker of history.

"But it pleases me merely to observe, to understand. I am purely a student of history—an amateur Toynbeean. I watch my ship of empire founder. If I were my father I would patch the sails, mend the ropes and beat out to clearer waters. But, since I am only myself, I must be satisfied to watch and to predict."

"Do you predict destruction, your majesty?" queried Shimatsu behind narrowing eyes.

"Destruction of what?" queried Juana-Maria. "The soul is indestructible, and that's all that's important to an old woman. As to whether my chancellor intends to destroy everything else . . ." She shrugged her fragile shoulders.

Shimatsu bowed, then murmured, "If your new super-secret bomb is as good as our agents say, we have no defense against it. And if we have no defense we must meet the attack of Haze-Gaunt with our own attack as long as we are able. And we have two advantages over you imperials.

"You are so certain that you have an overwhelming balance of force that you have never troubled to evaluate the weapons that may be used against you. Also, you have assumed that we must wait politely and let you choose the moment. May I suggest, your majesty, and gentlemen, that the Imperium is run, not by the famed 'wolf pack' but by credulous children?"

Donnan laughed uproariously. "There you have us!" he cried. "Credulous children!"

Shimatsu picked up the bear cape that he had been carrying over one arm and threw it around his shoulders in a gesture of finality. "You are amused, now. But when your zero hour draws close, prepare for a shock." He bowed deeply and passed on.

Alar knew that the man had issued a deadly warning.

"Now isn't that an odd coincidence?" observed Juana-Maria. "Dr. Talbot was telling me only a few minutes ago that the Imperium stands at this moment with the Assyrian Empire as of Six Hundred and Fourteen B.C. Perhaps Shimatsu knows whereof he speaks."

"What happened in Six Hundred and Fourteen B.C., Dr. Talbot?" asked Alar.

"The world's leading civilization was blasted to bits," replied the Toynbeean, stroking his goatee thoughtfully. "It's quite a story. For over two thousand years the Assyrians had fought to rule the world as they knew it. By Six Hundred and Fourteen B.C. the Assyrian ethos dominated an area extending from Jerusalem to Lydia. Four years later not one Assyrian city remained standing. Their destruction was so complete that when Xenophon led his Greeks by the ruins of Nineveh and Calah two centuries later, no one could tell him who had lived in them."

"That's quite a knockout, Dr. Talbot," agreed Alar. "But how do you draw a parallel between Assyria and America Imperial?"

"There are certain infallible guides. In Toynbeean parlance they're called 'failure of self-determination,' 'schism in the body social' and 'schism in the soul.' These phases of course all follow the 'time of troubles,' 'universal state' and the 'universal peace.' These latter two, paradoxically, mark every civilization for death when it is apparently at its strongest."

Donnan grunted dubiously. "Amalgamated Nuclear closed at five hundred and six this morning. If you Toynbeeans think the Imperium is on the skids you're the only ones."

Dr. Talbot smiled. "We Toynbeeans agree with you. Yet we don't try to force our opinions on the public, for two reasons. In the first place Toynbeeans only *study* history—they don't make it. In the second place nobody can stop an avalanche."

Donnan remained unconvinced. "You long-haired boys are always getting lost in what happened in ancient times. This is here and now—America Imperial, June Sixth, Two Thousand One Hundred Seventy-seven. We got the Indian sign on the world."

Dr. Talbot sighed. "I hope to God you're right, Senator."

Juana-Maria said, "If I may interrupt . . ."

The group bowed.

"The Senator may be interested in learning that for the past eight months the Toynbeeans have devoted themselves to but one project—a re-examination of their main thesis that all civilizations follow the same inevitable sociologic pattern. Am I right, Dr. Talbot?"

"Yes, your majesty. Like other human beings we want

to be right. But in our hearts we hope rather desperately that we'll be proved wrong. We grasp at any straw. We examine the past to learn if there weren't some instances where the universal state was not followed by destruction.

"We search for examples of civilizations that endured despite spiritual stratification. We look at the history of slavery to see whether the enslaving society ever escaped retribution.

"We compare our time of troubles—the Crises—with the Punic Wars that reduced the sturdy Roman farmer class to slavery and we study the Civil War of our North American ancestors over the slavery question. We consider then how long the Spartan Empire continued after the Peloponnesian War ground its once proud soldiery into serfdom.

"We seek comparisons in the past for our divided allegiance between the ancestor-worship taught our boys and girls in the Imperial Schools and the monotheism followed by our older people. We know what a divided spiritualism did to the Periclean Greeks, the Roman Empire, the budding Scandinavian society, the Celts of Ireland and the Nestorian Christians.

"We compare our present political schism—the Thieves versus the Government—with the bitterly opposed but unrepresented minorities that finally erased the Ottoman Empire, the Austro-Hungarian League and the Later Indic society, as well as various other civilizations.

"But we have found no exceptions to the pattern so far."

"You mentioned the institution of slavery several times as though it were undermining the Imperium," objected Donnan. "How do you arrive at that conclusion?"

"The rise of slavery in the Imperium precisely parallels its rise in Assyria, Sparta, Rome and all the other slave-holding empires," answered Talbot carefully. "No culture can aggrandize its ruling classes generation after generation without impoverishing its peasantry. Eventually these wretches are left with no assets except their own bodies.

"They are swallowed up by their richer brethren under contracts of bondage. Since their produce is not their own they have no means to better the lot of their numerous progeny and a perpetual slave class is born. The present population of the Imperium is over one and a half billion. One third of these souls are slaves."

"True," agreed Donnan, "but they don't really have such a hard lot. They have enough to eat, and a place to sleep—something a great many freemen don't have."

"That, of course," observed Juana-Maria dryly, "is a great recommendation for both free enterprise and for the slave system. To buy bread for his starving children, their father can always sell them to the highest bidder. But we're getting off the main track. Will there be a Toynbee Twenty-two?"

"We hope, your majesty. But, of course, a mere historian can make no guarantees."

"If there is to be a Twenty-two," she continued, "how would it differ from, say, our present Toynbee Twenty-one?"

"We think Twenty-two would successfully challenge our present drive to suicide," said Dr. Talbot simply.

"Interesting. To take it a little further, let us look back a bit. The Egyptaic Society was brought in by Imhotep, the Sinic by Confucius, the Andean by Virachoa, the Sumerian by Gilgamesh, the Islamic by Mohammed, and so on. Will a specific person usher in Twenty-two?"

The savant's eyes sparkled with admiration. "Your majesty is well read. But the answer isn't clear cut. Some civilizations are 'brought in,' as you say, by a given person. But many of them were not. Many are clearly group efforts."

"So we're back to groups," said the old woman. "How do you evaluate a given group, Dr. Talbot? How do you determine what cultural samples to take and what weight to give each?"

"The historian can evaluate his own society only as a weighted synthesis of its microcosmic components," admitted Talbot, tugging again at his goatee. "He can establish at best a probability as to the stage it has reached in the invariant pattern for civilizations. However, when he studies group after group, as I have, from the noblest families— your pardon, your majesty—right down to the bands of escaped slaves in the waste provinces of Texas and Arizona—"

"Ever studied the thieves, Dr. Talbot?" interrupted Alar.

The Wolf Pack

7

THE TOYNBEEAN STUDIED the masked man curiously. "The Thieves are unapproachable, of course, but the Society is just a rubber stamp of Kennicot Muir and I knew him well some years before he was killed. He realized all along that the Imperium was living on borrowed time."

"But how about our tiny settlements on the Moon, Mercury and the Sun?" insisted Alar. "There you ought to find enough vaulting optimism to negate the whole of the fatalism you've found here on Earth."

"For our Lunar Observatory Station I expect that's true," agreed Talbot, "assuming that you consider them as an independent society separate from the lunar fortifications. The morale of the few hundred men there should be high, owing to the flood of knowledge that continues to flow into the two-hundred meter reflector.

"The Mercury station is of course purely derivative of the solar stations and stands or falls with them. Your suggestion is interesting, because it so happens the Toynbeeans have finally received permission from Minister of War Eldridge to let one of our staff visit a solarion on the sun for twenty days, and I have been selected to go."

"How delightful!" exclaimed the Imperatrix. "What do you expect to find?"

"The very apotheosis of our civilization," replied Talbot gravely, "with all pretense and indirection thrown to the winds. Our present day phase of civilization, you know, we refer to as Toynbee Twenty-one. It is, of course, an attempt to categorize an extremely complex situation with the exclusion of irrelevant factors. But the solarions are unique. They are most directly a product purely of our own day. Specifically, I expect to find in Solarion Nine the distilled essence of Toynbee Twenty-one—thirty madmen hell-bent on suicide."

Intriguing, thought the Thief, but academic as far as he personally was concerned. He never expected to visit a solarion. "Could we take it one step further," he said. "What is the absolute minimum sample for a highly restricted zone? Say—a space ship?"

"We've worked it out on the computer," said Talbot. "According to the extrapolations, three is the minimum that would demonstrate significant societal change."

"Change to what?" persisted Alar.

"One degenerates, one progresses."

"The third?"

"The third dies."

Alar heard the last few words only perfunctorily, because his heartbeat was accelerating alarmingly. Shey, Thurmond, and a man he took to be Haze-Gaunt were passing by his elbow. He turned his back and shrank toward the wall.

The three paid him no attention whatever but walked rapidly toward the orchestra pit. From the corner of his eye Alar saw Thurmond say something to the conductor. The music stopped.

"May I apologize for this interruption, my lords and ladies?" came the chancellor's rich baritone over the speakers. "A very dangerous enemy of the Imperium is believed to be in the ballroom at this moment. I must ask, therefore, that all men who have not already done so remove their masks in order that the police may apprehend the intruder. This need not mar nor delay our festivities! On with the dance!" The chancellor nodded to the conductor and the great orchestra crashed into *Taya of Tehuantepec.*

An excited buzz sprang up everywhere as the bright-plumaged males began removing their masks and looking about the room. Gradually the couples were reabsorbed on the dance floor. As Alar slid along the wall his hand went to his mask, then dropped slowly. His strange heart began to beat even faster.

Several things were clamoring for his attention. The dancers were now taking notice of him even in the shadowed portion of the tapestried wall where he leaned. From the air, it seemed, several men in gray with I.P. service sabers crystallized a few feet from him on either side.

They were just standing their quietly, seemingly absorbed in the whirling gaiety. Two more leaned unobtrusively against a great column some twelve feet ahead. Alar's brown Thief mask was about as inconspicuous here as a red rag in front of a bull. He must have been mad to wear it.

His tongue worked dryly in his mouth. He carried an unfamiliar blade. He was exhausted—living on pure nervous energy. Even if his roving eyes could spot an exit opening on the gardens, he wasn't at all sure he could break out unscathed.

"*Your mask, sir?*"

It was Thurmond—standing squarely before him, hand on rapier pommel.

For a long, horrid moment the Thief thought his legs would give way and drop him to the marble flagging. At best he could not avoid the reflex action of licking his lips.

The police minister's feral eyes missed nothing. His mouth curled faintly. "Your mask, sir?" he repeated softly.

The man must have approached him from behind the column, and made one of the shadowy catleaps for which he was famous—and feared. He was drawing his blade slowly, seeming to take an almost sensuous pleasure in the Thief's rapid breathing.

"*Faut-il s'éloigner le masque? Pourquoi?*" asked Alar huskily. "*Qu'êtes-vous?*"

The barest shadow of doubt crossed Thurmond's face. But his blade was now out. Its point flashed even in the subdued light of the ballroom. "The chancellor would still like a conference with you," continued Thurmond. "If I can't arrange that, I'm to kill you. Conferences are just so much idle chatter and you might get lost on the way. So I'm going to kill you. Here. Now."

Alar finally got a deep breath.

There were other flashes of steel around him now. The gray men along the wall had drawn their blades and were sidling toward him. Two or three couples had stopped dancing and were staring in fascination at his approaching murder.

A blur! And Thurmond was suddenly one step closer. It was simply impossible for a human being to move so fast. It was clear now why poor Corrips—no mean swordsman—had lasted but seconds before the slashing wizardry of Giles Thurmond. And yet the man held back. Why? That phony diplomatic French must have removed his one-hundred-per-cent certainty. Thurmond evidently did not intend to kill him until the mask was off.

"*Vous m'insulte, tovarich,*" clipped Alar. "*Je vous demande encore, pourquoi dois-je déplacer le masque? Qu'êtes-vous? Je demande votre identité. Si vous désirez un duel, mes séconds—*"

Thurmond hesitated. "*Il faut déplacer le masque,*" he said curtly, "*parceque il y a un énémi de l'état au bal. C'est mon devoir, de l'apprendre. Alors, monsieur, s'il vous plaît, le masque—*"

The police minister had now taken care of the one-in-a-million possibility that Alar was actually a visiting dignitary who had not understood the chancellor's announcement. He was now ready to kill the Thief whether or not he removed his mask.

Alar's mind began to float in that curiously detached

way that ignored time. His heart, he noted, had leveled off at 170. Within one or two seconds he would be impaled by Thurmond's blade against the thick tapestries, writhing like an insect. That was no way for a Thief to die.

"*Madame, messieurs!*" he bowed in utter gratitude. Keiris had rounded the column with the chancellor and Ambassador Shimatsu on either arm. Thurmond's blade, an inch in front of his heart, wavered.

"*Madame,*" continued the Thief smoothly, "*voulez-vous expliquer à cet homme mon identité?*"

Keiris's eyes were wide with something nameless. This moment, one that she had dreaded for years, had finally come. If she saved the life of the Thief her double life must soon be discovered. What would happen to her then? Would Haze-Gaunt sell her to Shey?

She said quietly, "You have made a grave mistake, General Thurmond. May I introduce Dr. Hallmarck, of the University of Kharkov?"

Alar bowed. Thurmond sheathed his weapon slowly. It was clear that he was unconvinced.

Shimatsu, too, was studying Alar dubiously. He started to speak, then hesitated, finally said nothing.

Haze-Gaunt fixed hard eyes on the Thief. "We are honored sir. But as a matter of courtesy, it might be well to—"

"*Comment, monsieur?*" Alar shrugged his shoulders. "*Je ne parle pas l'anglais. Veuillez, madame, voulez-vous traduire?*"

The woman laughed artificially and turned to the chancellor. "The poor dear doesn't know what it's all about. He has this dance with me. I'll get his mask from him. And you really ought to be more careful, General Thurmond."

She was talking before they were well away. "I doubt that you can escape now," she said hurriedly. "But your best chance will be to do exactly as I say. Remove your mask immediately."

He did so, placed it in his jacket pocket. She had maneuvered him carefully, so that he faced away from the chancellor's group.

His arm was around her now and they glided in a slow whirl across the room. To have her so close, with her body continuously touching his, reactivated the tantalizing memory syndrome of the balcony—only now it was doubled, redoubled.

He was not much taller than she and his nostrils once got buried in the fine black hair at her temple. Even its odor was exasperatingly familiar. Had he known this woman at some time in his phantom past? No way to tell. She had given no hint of recognition.

"Whatever you have in mind," he urged nervously, "do it quickly. As we left them Shimatsu was telling Haze-Gaunt that I spoke English. That's all Thurmond needs."

They were through the milling crowd now and in the shadowed fountain gallery.

"I can't go any further, Alar," said the woman rapidly. "At the end of this corridor is a refuse chute. It will drop you into one of the incinerator pits in the bowels of the palace. The incinerators will be fired at any moment but you'll have to take the chance. You'll find friends in a great vault adjoining the incinerators. Are you afraid?"

"A little. But who are these 'friends'?"

"Thieves. They're building a strange space-ship."

"The *T-twenty-two*? But that's an imperial project. It's guarded tighter than a drum. The Under-secretary for Space, Gaines, is in charge himself."

"Two I.P.'s are coming up the hall," she countered quickly. "They're sure about you now. You'll have to run for it."

"Not yet. They think I'm cornered and they'll wait for reinforcements. In the meantime, what about you? Haze-Gaunt isn't going to like this." His hands were on her shoulders. They looked at each other silently a moment, bonded by their unknown and dangerous features.

"I'm not afraid of *him*. It's Shey, the psychologist. He

knows how to hurt people so that they will tell him whatever he wants to know. Sometimes I think he tortures just for the sake of seeing suffering. He wants to buy me—for that—but so far Haze-Gaunt hasn't let him touch me. Whatever you do, avoid Shey."

"All right, I'll keep away from him. But why are you doing this for me?"

"You remind me of someone I used to know," replied the woman slowly. She looked behind her. "For God's sake, hurry!"

His fingers tightened insistently on her shoulders. "Who is this person I remind you of?" he cried harshly.

"Run!"

He had to.

Within seconds he was at the chute-door, flashing frantic fingers over it. There was no handle. The rush of feet sounded just behind him. Of course there was no handle— the thing was hinged inward.

He plunged into the narrow blackness and was swirled around and around as he shot down. If he crashed into a pile of anything solid at this velocity, he would certainly break both legs. In the very act of trying to slow his descent by turning out his knees and elbows, he hurtled through the darkness into a mass of something foul and yielding. Nothing was hurt but his dignity. He was on his feet almost before the clouds of dust began to rise.

The blackness was complete, save for a beam of light from one side of the incinerator that was his prison. It was apparently the operator's peephole in the charging door. He stumbled over to the peephole, blinked and peered out.

The great room was deserted.

He rattled the door cautiously, and tried the iron drop-latch.

It was locked from outside.

The Thief wiped his forehead with his sleeve, drew his saber and pried tentatively at the lock mechanism. It was too solid.

The soft grate of steel on steel echoed mockingly within the narrow confines of the incinerator as he replaced the weapon.

He had begun to feel his way slowly around his prison when he heard footsteps on the concrete floor outside.

The furnace door opened and a mass of flaming rubble sailed past his horrified eyes.

The door clanged shut just as he leaped to smother the torch with his chest.

The shaft of light was gone. A slave janitor was probably peering into the darkness, and wondering.

The Thief heard a muffled curse, then the sound of fading footsteps. He was at the door instantly.

The slave ought to be back in a minute or two.

And he was. This time the ignition wad was larger. The peephole was closed a long time as the slave made sure the charge was burning properly. Finally he went away. The Thief removed his saber point from the lock engagement and eased the door open. Cold air rushed into his scorched lungs and over his blistered face.

He was on the floor instantly, and forced himself to take time to close and relock the door. Precious seconds were gone, but it might delay his pursuers if they had to look in every incinerator for him.

He vanished, wraithlike, between the bulge of two furnaces, heading toward the west wing and the fabulous *T-twenty-two*.

Was the brilliant Gaines really a Thief? If he were, did that mean that Haze-Gaunt's government was riddled with members of the Society?

Two things were certain. The wolf pack knew a great deal about him. To them he was something more than *a* Thief. And the Society of Thieves had placed an incredible value on his life. Furthermore, Haven knew as much, or more, about him than the wolf pack. He had some pressing questions to ask him if ever he saw his friend again.

He opened the door to the great vault chamber a quarter of an inch and peered along the inner wall. Nothing moved. From far away, toward the center of the chamber, he heard the hiss of the nucleic welders.

Very quietly he slipped inside the door—and sucked in his breath sharply.

Even in the dusky gloom the *T-twenty-two* shimmered with a pale blue haze. Her sleek, sheer flanks shot fifty meters into the air, but she was less than three meters in diameter at her waist. A great moon freighter would make several hundred of her.

But the thing that troubled him, the thing that seized his mind and blanked out the trip-hammering of his heart, was this—He had seen the *T-twenty-two* before—*years* before.

Even as the sandbag crashed into his head, and even as he clawed futilely toward consciousness, he could only think—*T-twenty-two*—*T-twenty-two*—where—when?

Discovery through Torment

8

H E'S REGAINING CONSCIOUSNESS," sniggered the voice.

Alar sat up on one knee and peered out from aching eyes.

He was in a large cage of metal bars, barely tall enough for him to stand. The cage stood in the center of a large stone-walled room. All about him was a raw, musty odor. The rawness, he realized with quivering nostrils, was blood. In these rooms the imperial psychologist practiced his inhuman arts.

"Good morning, Thief!" burbled Shey, rising up and down on tiptoe.

Alar tried in vain to swallow, then struggled to his feet. For the first time in his life he was thankful that he was utterly exhausted. In the long hours that would follow he could faint easily and frequently.

"It has been suggested to me," chirped Shey, "that with proper stimulation you might demonstrate powers not before known in human beings—hence the iron cage that now holds you. We would like to see a good performance—but without danger to ourselves or the risk of losing you."

Alar was silent. Protests would avail him nothing. Furthermore, it would not improve things for Shey to recognize the voice of the Thief who had so recently robbed him.

71

The psychologist drew closer to the cage. "Pain is a wonderful thing, you know," he whispered eagerly. He rolled up his right sleeve. "See these scars? I held hot knives there as long as I could. The stimulation—ah!" He inhaled ecstatically. "But you'll soon know, won't you? My difficulty is that I always release the knife before I attain maximum stimulation. But with someone else to help as *I* shall help *you*—" He smiled engagingly. "I hope you won't disappoint us."

Alar felt something cold crawl slowly up his spine.

"Now," continued the psychologist, "will you hold out your arm and let the attendant give you an injection or do you prefer that we crush you between the cage walls to administer it? Just a harmless bit of adrenalin so you won't faint—for a long, long time."

There was nothing to be done. And in a way he was even more curious than Shey as to what would happen. He thrust out his arm in grim silence and the needle jammed home.

The phone buzzed. "Answer that," ordered Shey.

"It's from upstairs," called the attendant. "They want to know if you've seen Madame Haze-Gaunt."

"Tell them no."

Additional attendants wheeled up a heavy hinged case, opened it and began to take things from it and to lay them on the table. Still others rolled the cage walls together, flattening the Thief like a bacillus between microscope slides.

Alar listened vaguely to the sweat plashing from his chin to the stone floor, providing an insane obbligato to the strumming of an adrenalin-fed heart. From behind him somewhere wafted the odor of red-hot metal.

At least Keiris had got away.

It was twilight and, because there was no longer any pain, he thought for a moment that he was dead. Then he stood up and looked about him in wonder. In this world he was the only moving thing.

He was suspended in space near a silent, winding column. Gravity was banished here. There was no up, no down, no frame of reference for direction, so the column was neither necessarily vertical nor horizontal. He rubbed his eyes. The physical contact of palm to face seemed real. This was no dream. Some enormous soul-shaking thing had happened to him that he could not fathom. Here there was no movement, no sound, nothing but the column and vast brooding silence.

Gingerly he reached out to touch the column. It had a strangely fluid, pliant quality, like a ray of light bending. And it had a strange shape. The part that he touched was a five-finned flange that extended from the central portion of the column.

If he had a power saw, he thought, how simple it would be to saw out innumerable arms with hands and fingers. Touching the flange lightly, he floated around the column to the other side, where he found an identical five-finned arrangement. He frowned, perplexed. Farther around the column were leg-like fins.

His eyes brightened as he realized that a cross-section of this column would resemble very closely the vertical cross section of a human being. Looking about, he discovered that the column appeared to go on indefinitely.

He then floated along it in the opposite direction for some minutes, noting that it gradually grew smaller in cross section. The cheek outline was thinner, the bones more prominent. The outline might be that of a skinny youth. Even farther on, the column was still smaller, and, by straining his eyes, he thought he could see where it shrank to a thread in the distance.

The Thief believed his life depended on the solution to this mystery, but cast about as he might, the answer eluded him.

He returned slowly, pensively, and studied the column at approximately the point where he had found himself when he recovered consciousness. He knotted his jaws in exasperation.

Perhaps the interior of the column held an explanation.

He thrust an arm into it slowly, and noted with interest that some plastic force seemed to draw his fingers into the five-finned portion of the column. He stuck in his right leg. That fitted perfectly.

Tentatively, he eased the rest of his body into the column.

And then something immense and elemental seized him and flung him—

"He's regaining consciousness," sniggered the voice.

Alar sat up on one knee and peered out from aching eyes.

His head was whirling. He was in the center of the cage, not crushed between the walls. There was no blood on him anywhere and somehow his shirt and coat had got back on him. Everything—the position of the men, the table, the instruments—were in the same places as when he first awakened in the cage an infinity ago, before the injection and the pain.

Had the pain really been just a nightmare, topped off by that queer episode of the man-shaped column? Was it just an illusionary *déja vu* to expect Shey to rise up and down on tiptoe and burble—

"Good morning, Thief!" burbled Shey, rising up and down on tiptoe.

Alar felt the blood draining from his face.

He understood one thing very clearly. Through means utterly incomprehensible to him he had, for a time, left the time stream and had re-entered it at the worst possible locus. He knew that this time his resolution would falter—that he would talk and that his comrades would die. And he had no weapon, no means to prevent this catastrophe that was finally upon him.

Except—his heart bounded in fierce joy and he listened to his calm icy voice. "I think that you will release me very soon."

Shey shook his curly head in rare good humor. "That

would spoil everything. No, I won't release you for a long time. I might even say—never."

Alar's lips compressed in a chill confidence he was far from feeling. Speed was utterly essential. He must get in his point before the telephone rang. Yet he must not seem hurried or anxious. Shey was sure to recognize his voice but that couldn't be helped.

He folded his arm across his chest and leaned against the back bars. "I am perhaps overvalued by the Society of Thieves," he said shortly. "Be that as it may. Still, certain precautions have been taken against my capture and I must warn you that if I do not leave the palace safely within ten minutes the corpse of Madame Haze-Gaunt will be delivered to the chancellor tonight."

Shey frowned and studied his quarry thoughtfully. "That voice—Hmm. You're lying, of course—just trying to gain time. Her excellency is still on the ballroom floor. Your shortened breathing, narrrowed pupils, dry voice—all point to a deliberate lie. I won't even check on it. Now, will you hold out your arm, please, for a little shot of adrenalin?"

Wasn't the phone ever going to ring?

His continued calm exterior amazed him. "Very well," he murmured, thrusting out his arm. "We three die together." The needle jabbed in and struck a nerve. Alar's face twitched faintly. The attendants rolled the cage walls together, flattening the Thief spread-eagle fashion.

The odor of heating metal was strong behind him. His head was beginning to spin. Something was wrong. But for the bars crushing him he knew he would drop. Wet circles of sweat were spreading slowly from the armpits of his jacket.

Two burly attendants wheeled up the instrument chests. Alar forced himself to watch them casually as they opened it and handed a strange-shaped pair of pliers to Shey.

A shudder of nausea crept up Alar's throat as he remembered his bloody nail-less hand-things from—that other time.

"Do you know," chuckled Shey as he fixed a coy eye on Alar, "I believe you're the chap that called on me a few nights ago."

The phone buzzed.

Shey looked up absently. "Answer that," he ordered dreamily.

Time ground slowly to a halt for the Thief. His chest was heaving in great gasps.

"It's from upstairs," called the attendant hesitantly. "They want to know if you've seen Madame Haze-Gaunt."

Shey waited a long time before answering. His look of introspection died away slowly. Finally he turned around and carefully replaced the nail pullers in the chest.

"Tell them no," he said, "and get the chancellor on the phone for me instantly."

Alar was left at the busy downtown intersection as he had demanded and, after an hour of careful wandering to elude possible I.P. tailers, he walked via alley and cellar to the door of the Society rendezvous. Before he slept, ate or even got a new blade, he wanted to lay before the Council the incredible occurrences in the slave underground and in Shey's torture chamber.

Something sharp jabbed into his side. He raised his hands slowly to find himself surrounded by masked Thieves with drawn blades. The man wielding the nearest saber stated, "You are under arrest."

"Y OU ARE NOW under a sentence of death," intoned the masked man on the dais. "In accordance with the laws of the Society the charges against you will be read, and you will then be given ten minutes to present your defense. At the end of that time, if you have failed to refute the charges against you beyond a reasonable doubt, you will be put to death with a rapier thrust through your heart. The clerk of this tribunal will read the charge."

Alar could not free his brain of a numbing dullness. He was too tired even to feel bewildered. Of all the Thieves here he recognized only Haven, whose stricken eyes peered out at him through a brown mask.

The masked clerk arose from a desk near the dais and read gravely. "Alar was captured by government operatives in the imperial palace approximately four hours ago, taken to the lower chambers and delivered into the custody of Shey.

"A few minutes later he was escorted unscathed from the palace to the street and there released. In view of his unbroken skin it is presumed that the prisoner disclosed confidential information concerning the Society. The charge is treason, the sentence death."

"Fellow Thieves!" Haven sprang to his feet. "I object to

this procedure. The burden of proof of betrayal ought to be on the Society. In the past Alar has risked his life for the Society many times. I now urge that we give him the benefit of the doubt. Let us presume him innocent until we have proved him guilty."

Alar studied the sea of masks confronting him. The judge listened to several men who bent toward him and whispered. Finally the judge straightened up. Alar's nails dug into the wooden rails. He knew he could prove nothing.

"Number eighty-nine," said the judge slowly, "has proposed a radical innovation in trial procedure. In the past, the Society has found it necessary to liquidate Thieves who have been unable to free themselves from suspicion. Trial boards of the Society unanimously agree that by this method we destroy more innocent men than guilty.

"That price, I feel, is small, if it ensures the continuation of the Society as a whole. The question now is—are there any special circumstances that indicate the ends of the Society will best be served by a reversal of the burden of proof?"

Alar listened to his pulse-rate mount slowly. One seventy-five . . . one eighty . . .

"There are unusual, even strange, circumstances in this case," continued the judge, leafing slowly through the brochure before him. "But all of them"—he transfixed Alar with steely eyes and hardening voice—"all of them indicate that we should redouble our care in dealing with this man, rather than lessen it.

"He is unable to account for his life prior to one night five years ago when, as an ostensible amnesiac, he found shelter with two members of this Society. And we must keep in mind that Chancellor Haze-Gaunt would be sufficiently ingenious to attempt to plant an agent provocateur among us by just such a ruse.

"When Alar emerged safely from the clutches of Shey we were entitled to suspect the worst. Does the defendant deny that he stands here among us with a whole skin when by rights he should be dead or dying?" The voice was faintly ironic.

"I neither deny nor affirm anything," replied Alar. "But before I begin a defense, I would like to ask a question. Since the sentence is death and I cannot leave this room alive, perhaps the judge will be willing to tell me why the Society protected me when I was a helpless amnesiac and why, after permitting me to lead the dangerous life of a Thief, Dr. Haven and Dr. Corrips suddenly decided my life was more important than some twenty-odd brilliant minds in the Geotropic Project at the University. Without regard to what has—or has not—happened since, you must admit the stand is inconsistent."

"Not necessarily," replied the judge coldly. "But you may form your own opinion. Five years ago a strange space ship crashed into the upper Ohio River. Certain flotsam was recovered from the wreckage that indicated it must have come from outer space. Two living things were recovered from it. One was a strange ape-like animal later captured by the River Police and given to Haze-Gaunt. The other was—you. We immediately got a note from Kennicot Muir concerning your disposition."

"But he's dead!" interjected Alar.

The judge smiled grimly. "He is thought to be dead by the Imperial Government and by the world outside. As I say, we got a note from him to the effect that you were to be enrolled in the Society as soon as your emotional pattern was stabilized. You were to be given routine assignments involving but little physical danger, and you were to be studied.

"It was Muir's opinion that possibly you were a species of man of rather special properties—that your ancestral line had evolved beyond homo sapiens into something that could be of immense help to us in averting the impending Operations Finis that Haze-Gaunt may launch at any hour. Very early we discovered that your heart accelerates before you consciously detect danger.

"We know now that your subconscious mind synthesizes impressions and stimuli of which your conscious mind is unaware, and prepares your body for the unseen peril, whatever it is. This was good but not good enough for us to place you beyond homo sapiens or to absolve you completely from suspicion as a planted spy.

"We waited for other manifestations of your possible ultra-humanity but nothing more was forthcoming. And after your probable treachery tonight, your threat to the existence of the Society outweighs its desire to continue studying you."

So his earlier life would soon be sealed forever. Did no one know? He demanded, "Is Muir present now? Does he agree to my death?"

"Muir is not present, and as a matter of fact none of us has seen him in the flesh since his disappearance. But you can be sure he knows of this trial. So far he has not disagreed. Do you have any more questions? If not, the time for your defense must begin to run. You have ten minutes."

With pale face Alar studied his executioners. Many of them must have shared perilous adventures with him but would now kill him willingly to save the Society. His heartbeat was mounting steadily. Two hundred. It had never been so high.

"Any defense"—his coolness amazed him—"that I might bring forward would be so implausible and incredible from the point of view of most of you that it would be a waste of precious minutes to attempt any explanation whatever. If I have ten minutes to live—"

"Nine," corrected the clerk firmly.

"Then I intend to use them to save my life. John!"

"Yes, boy?" Haven's voice shook a little.

"John, if you believe that I am innocent, please explain this to me—what is the chemical basis of eyesight?"

The biologist looked startled but instantly recovered his poise. Blood began to flood back into his cheeks. "It is generally agreed," he declared, "that photons reflected from the thing being viewed enter the pupil of the eye and are focussed as they pass through the vitreous and aqueous humors to the retina, where an image is formed.

"There they impinge upon the visual purple, which then gives off a substance to which the retinal rods and cones are sensitive. The rods and cones pass the stimulus on to the retinal nerve endings, which gather finally into the great optic nerve and register the image in the crevasses of the optic lobe at the base of the brain."

"Would you say that it is quite impossible for the reverse of that process to occur?"

"Reverse? You mean, where the brain conceives an image, passes it along the optic nerve to the retina, and the visual purple is so stimulated that it releases photons that are focussed by the eyes' refractive fluids to project an image? Do you mean to ask whether your eyes may be capable of projecting an image as well as receiving one? Is that what you mean?"

"Precisely. Is it impossible?"

The men strained forward in puzzled attention.

"You have three minutes," reminded the clerk sharply, looking from Alar to Haven and back again.

Haven fixed eyes wide with surmise on his protégé. "Visual projection has been predicted for the creature that may follow homo sapiens in the evolutionary scale. This power may evolve within the next fifty or a hundred millennia. But now, in modern man? Highly improbable.

"However"—he raised a warning hand in a gesture full of hidden meaning—"if someone *were* able to project light beams from his eyes—if he were able to do that he ought to be able to reverse other stimulus-response systems. For example, he should be able to turn the tympanum of the ear into a speech membrane, by activation of the cochlear nerves with the cerebral auditory tract. In a word, he should be able to reproduce aurally—not orally—any sound he can imagine!"

Alar stole a glance at the dim fluorescent tube in the ceiling fixture. A warm flush crept quickly up his throat. He knew now that he would live and not die—that he would live to unravel the gray net that enshrouded his past—that he would leave the Thieves and that he would henceforth search for himself in earnest. But there was much to be done yet, and he was far from being out of danger. He awakened to the voice of the judge:

"What did you hope to accomplish by that senseless discussion with Dr. Haven? Only thirty seconds of time remain for your defense."

Around him there was the eerie sliding of finely wrought steel on steel. All the Thieves except Haven had drawn their blades and were watching him with feline intentness.

Alar stared upward at the ancient fluorescent light. It reminded him of the searchlight beam glowing through the dust cloud when he was trapped that time in the slave underground. There was no more mystery now about his escape then. He knew the explanation for the figure in the tattered coat, the figure that appeared to be his own. The figure had indeed been his own. It had been an image of his own body projected on the settling dust. He had not known the extent of his ability to reverse his stimulus-response system, and yet, subconsciously, with the wish to see himself escape he had created a photic image of himself—and the wish had been fulfilled.

He closed one eye and concentrated feverishly on the dim tube in the ceiling, trying to reawaken his wonderful power. This time it might save him again, although in a different way. If he could only impinge enough photons of the proper quanta and frequency on the fluorescent coating of the lamp, he believed he could fill in the troughs of the emitted photonwaves and throw the room into darkness.

The light seemed to flicker a little.

His breath was like that of a panting dog and sweat was streaming into his open eye. A few feet in front of him a

Thief raised his blade level with Alar's heart and sighted along it coolly.

Haven's nervous whisper rasped behind him. "Fluorescent light is higher on the spectrum. Raise your frequency a little."

The executioner lunged at him.

The room went dark.

Alar held his left hand over the nasty cut in his chest and slipped away a few feet. Not far—he had to stay in the open in order to control the lamp. Life now would depend on the boldest improvisation.

No one had moved. All around him came the accelerated expectant breathing of the men who wanted to kill him—as soon as they could distinguish his dark form from themselves.

Then—

His right ear heard sounds coming from his left ear:

"Let no one move! Alar must still be in the room. We'll find him as soon as we have a light. Number twenty-fourteen, go immediately to the outer office and obtain emergency lighting." It was a reasonable facsimile of the judge's voice. The danger was, did the judge think so too?

Alar backed off quickly two paces and said in muffled tones, "Yes, sir."

How soon would it take someone to remember that Number twenty-fourteen was stationed down the corridor?

Again the tense silence as he edged backward towards the door. It was a fantastically difficult task to avoid cutting off his view of the lamp. He pushed fellow Thieves apologetically out of the way as he stumbled ever backwards. But only one man need walk in front of his line of vision and his control of the lamp would vanish in a blaze of light. A dozen blades would cut him down.

He sensed the door now beside him, the guard in front of it.

"Who is it?" The guard's tense question shot from the dark, a bare foot away.

"Twenty-fourteen," Alar whispered quickly. He could feel warm blood trickling down his leg. He must find bandages soon.

A heated, sibilant argument was in progress somewhere in the room. He caught the word "twenty-fourteen" once.

"Your honor!" called someone nasally.

He listened to the guard hesitate in the very act of sliding back the bolts. His hoax would be exposed in seconds. "Hurry up!" he whispered impatiently.

"You have the floor!" called the judge to the nasal Thief.

The guard stood motionless, listening.

"If Alar escapes because of your delay," hissed Alar to him, "you'll be responsible."

But the man stood immobile.

Again that nasal voice from the other side of the room—"Your honor, some of us are of the understanding that Number twenty-fourteen is actually stationed at the far end of the exit corridor. If this is so your orders that he leave the room must have been answered by Alar!"

It was out.

"*My* orders? came the astounded reply. "*I* gave no orders. I thought it was the sergeant of the guard! Door guard! Let no one whatever leave the room!"

The bolts clanged shut before him with grim finality. With a last despairing blast of mental effort Alar reactivated the dampened fluorescent bulb with a shaft of dazzling blue light.

Pandemonium broke loose.

A split second later he had knocked down the blinded guard, drawn the bolts and was out while a score of men groped inside. But their retinal over-stimulation would wear off quickly and he must hurry. He looked up the corridor. Number twenty-fourteen and his detail blocked that path. He knotted his fists, then turned to study the dead end of the corridor behind him—and his hand flew futilely to his empty scabbard.

Someone was standing there in the cul-de-sac.

"You can escape this way."

"Keiris!" he exclaimed softly.

"You'd best come quickly."

He was immediately beside her. "But how—?"

"No questions now." She pushed open a narrow panel in the wall, and they stepped behind it just as the trial room burst open. They listened to the muffled but grim voices from beyond the panel.

"Don't underestimate them," whispered the woman, pulling him up the dark passage by the hand. "They'll question the guard up the corridor, then scour this end. They'll find the panel within sixty seconds."

Soon they were in a dim-lit alley at the first street level.

"What now?" he panted.

"My coupé is over there."

"So?"

She stopped and looked up at him gravely. "You are free for a little while, my friend, but your reason must tell you that you can expect to be caught within a matter of hours. The I.P.'s are combing the city for you, block by block, house by house, room by room.

"All roads from the city are closed. All non-police air-craft are grounded. And the Thieves are looking for you too. Their methods will be less gross but even more efficient. If you try to escape without a plan or without assistance the Thieves will certainly recapture you."

"I'm with you," he said shortly, taking her arm. They got into the coupé silently.

The gloomy alleyway began to race by them as the atom-powered rotors gathered speed.

"You'll find antibiotics and astringents in the first-aid kit," said the woman coolly. "You'll have to dress your wound yourself. Please do it quickly."

He ripped off his coat, shirt and underwear with blood-slippery fingers. The antibiotic powder stung and the astringent brought tears to his eyes. He slapped adhesive gauze over the wound.

"You'll find more clothes in the bundle beside you."

He felt too weak to bring up the question of propriety. He unwrapped the bundle.

"You are in the process of assuming the identity of one Dr. Philip Ames, Astrophysicist," Keiris informed him.

Alar zipped up his new shirt in silence, then loosened his belt and changed his trousers.

"Actually," continued the woman tersely, "Ames doesn't exist except in certain Government transcripts. The wallet in your inside coat pocket contains your new personal papers, a ticket for the next lunar flight and your sealed orders from the Imperial Astrophysics Laboratory, counter-signed by Haze-Gaunt."

There was some tremendous fact staring at him that he couldn't quite grasp. If only he weren't so tired. "I assume," he said slowly, "that the Imperial Laboratory knows that Haze-Gaunt is sending a man to Lunar, but doesn't know who is being sent. Otherwise, I would be exposed immediately as an impostor.

"I must assume, too, that Haze-Gaunt, if he has thought about it at all, believes he is sending an Imperial Astrophysicist whose identity is known only to him. Such double deception must have been planned and executed by a third person."

Now he had it!

And he was just as much in the dark as ever. He turned to the woman accusingly. "Only one intellect could have calculated the probability of my escape from Shey and where my trial by the Society would be held. Only one man could have controlled Haze-Gaunt's course of action in selecting 'Ames'—The Meganet Mind!"

"It was he."

Alar took a deep breath. "But why should he try to save the life of a Thief?"

"I'm not sure, but I think it's because he wants you to discover something vital at Lunar, something in a fragment of sky map. It's all in your orders. Besides, the Mind is a secret Thief sympathizer."

"I don't understand."

"Nor I. We weren't supposed to."

Alar felt completely lost, out of his depth. A few minutes before the world consisted neatly of Thieves and Imperials. Now he felt vividly the impact of a brain that treated both factions as children—an inconceivably deep brain that labored with infinite skill and patience toward—what?

"That's Lunar Terminus ahead," said his companion. "Your luggage has already been checked aboard. They'll examine your visa carefully but I don't think there'll be any trouble. If you want to change your mind this is your last chance."

Haze-Gaunt and the Imperial Laboratory would eventually get together and compare notes. A brief vision of being cornered by hard-bitten I.P.'s in the tiny Lunar Observatory settlement flashed into Alar's mind and his saber hand twitched uneasily.

And yet—just what *was* on the star plate? And why had the Meganet Mind picked *him* to discover it? Could it throw any light on his identity?

Of course he would go!

"Goodbye, then, Keiris," he said gently. "Incidentally there's something I ought to warn you about. It's known at the chancellory that you're missing right now. Don't ask me how I know. I just do. It will be very dangerous for you to return. Can't you come with me?"

She shook her head. "Not yet—not yet."

The Questioning

10

As SHE HURRIED up the secret stairway to her chancellory apartment, Keiris's calm exterior belied the tumult within her—the same tumult that had been raging from the moment Alar's lithe form had dropped over her window sill earlier in the evening. The armor that she had carefully built up around her since Kim's disappearance (was he really dead?) had fallen about her in ruins.

Why should an unknown Thief affect her this way?

His unmasked face had provided no clue. That was disappointing, because she never forgot a face. And yet her first glimpse of that rather broad soft face with the incongruously hard dark eyes, instead of dismissing the problem as nonexistent, had accentuated it.

She knew that she had never seen that face before. She also knew that he was utterly familiar—as much a part of her as the clothes she wore. Was that disloyal to Kim? It depended on how she meant it.

As she stood before the panel opening into her bathroom, she found herself blushing.

She shrugged her shoulders. No time now for analysis of personal feelings. Haze-Gaunt would be waiting for her in her bedroom, wondering where she'd been. Thank heaven for his fantastic jealousy. He'd only half-believe her anyway, but it provided a queer sort of security for her—a status quo consistently defined by its very insecurity.

She sighed and started sliding the panel back.

At least she'd have time to take a shower and have her women rub her down with rose petals. That would give her more time to invent answers for the questions that Haze-Gaunt would certainly ask. And then she'd squeeze into that low-necked—

"Have a pleasant outing?" asked Haze-Gaunt.

She would have screamed if her tongue hadn't stuck to the roof of her mouth. But she gave no exterior sign of shock. She got a full deep breath into her lungs and it was over.

She looked at the three intruders with outward calm. Haze-Gaunt was staring at her in gloomy uncertainty, legs spread, hands locked behind his back. Shey was beaming in happy anticipation. The deep lines in General Thurmond's face were, on the whole, noncommittal. Possibly the parentheses enclosing his small dash of a mouth looked a little harder, a little crueler.

Her heart beat faster. For the first time since Haze-Gaunt had placed her in his quarters she felt a thrill of physical fear. Her mind simply refused to accept the implications of Haze-Gaunt accompanied by the two most merciless monsters in the Imperium.

She had planned her most plausible line of defense even as Haze-Gaunt's question left his lips. Smiling wryly, she closed the panel behind her. "Yes, I had a pleasant outing, Bern. I go out whenever I can. Slaves have the vices of slaves, don't they?"

"We'll come back to that," rejoined the chancellor grimly. "The main question is, what do you know about Alar? How did you meet? Why did you let him escort you to the ball instead of turning him over to the palace guards?"

"Bern," she said, "is my bathroom the place for an inquisition? And it's really rather late. Perhaps in the morning."

She could have bitten off her tongue. This defense was not ringing true. She could sense the little psychologist anticipating her every word—knowing almost exactly what she would say next. Perhaps the diabolical little man had even forewarned Haze-Gaunt of what she could be expected to say if she were hiding something from them.

"Oh, very well," she said wearily, stepping away from the wall. "I'll tell you what I know, though I can't see why it's so important. Alar climbed up on my balcony this evening. I threw a knife at him but I wasn't a very good shot. I missed and in the next instant he had me by the wrist.

"He said he'd kill me if I didn't take him into the ballroom. What could I do? My maids were gone. It's really your fault, Bern, for not providing at least a minimum of protection for me."

She knew it was no good, but at least they'd take a few moments to pick it to pieces. Meanwhile, she would be thinking. She walked casually to the wash basin, as though she had made her final contribution to the discussion, and studied her face in the mirrors a few seconds. She was spraying her face with a perfumed water-palm oil emulsion when Haze-Gaunt spoke again.

"Your friend seems to have taken a shower in here and borrowed some of my clothes—not to mention the Italian saber. Were you bound and gagged during all that?"

Keiris stopped rubbing her oiled face and reached languidly for the water-alcohol spray knob. "It has always been my understanding that my apartment was wired with concealed microphones. I assumed that every word that passed between the Thief and me would be heard by the guards and that Alar would be captured in this very room."

"By a remarkable coincidence," Thurmond murmured, "your knife severed the wire."

The water-alcohol spray stung her cheeks sharply. She rubbed her face briskly with a deep-napped towel, then faced the three again with a shell of poise that was growing thinner by the minute.

Shey was still smiling. Once, he seemed almost to chuckle.

"I'll give you the benefit of the doubt on that," said Haze-Gaunt coldly. He unlaced his fingers from the small of his back and folded his arms on his chest as he sauntered toward them. "And I'll even assume, for the time being, that the next phase of your story is true—that you believed we knew all along that the Thief at the ball was Alar, and that we were biding our own good time in taking him. We'll let that go.

"You may or may not know that after his capture Alar was given to Shey for examination and that Alar somehow knew that you were missing from the palace grounds an hour ago, just before Shey was to have begun his experiments. Alar obtained his release by telling Shey that you were being held as a hostage by the Thieves. You must have told him that you would be missing at that moment, and that he could use the knowledge to effect his release. Do you deny that?"

Keiris hesitated and looked at Shey for the first time. The pain-dabbler was eyeing her in rapt anticipation. She knew that her face must be very pale. For nearly a decade she had thought she could face death with calm. But now that the probability was crystallizing before her very eyes it became horrible.

What was it about death that frightened her? Not death itself. Only the hour of dying—the hour that Shey knew how to prolong indefinitely. And she would talk. She knew that Shey could make her talk. She would have to tell about the Meganet Mind and a potent weapon would be lost for Kim's Thieves.

Somewhere, somehow, Kim might still be alive. What would he think when he learned of her betrayal? And incidentally, just how had Alar known that she had been waiting for him at the Thief rendezvous during his brief imprisonment in Shey's chambers? There were too many questions, and no answers.

She wondered just how much pain she could take before she became talkative.

"I deny nothing," she said finally. "If you want to think that I provided the Thief with the means for his escape you may certainly do so. Does my background lead you to expect an overwhelming loyalty to you, Bern?" She watched his face closely.

Haze-Gaunt was silent. Thurmond shifted his feet restlessly and glanced at his wrist radio.

"Haze-Gaunt," he clipped, "do you realize we're letting this woman hold up Operation Finis? Every second is vital if we are to achieve surprise, but we can do nothing until we evaluate Alar. I urge that you turn her over to Shey immediately. Her actions show something more than a generalized sympathy with a subversive organization that she identified with her late husband.

"There was something special between her and Alar. We must pull it out of her. And what about these incessant leaks of high secrets to the Thieves? You always thought you knew every move she made, every word she said. Where," he concluded tersely, "has she been for the last hour?"

"I have been with Alar." She found it incredible that her voice could be so calm. She watched for the effect of the statement on Haze-Gaunt. The barest flicker of anguish passed over his eternally immobile mouth.

She had been abandoned.

Shey giggled and spoke for the first time. "Your answers are so clear that they completely obscure—what? You point with sweeping gestures to a wide-open highway but it is the camouflaged path that we seek.

"Why are you so eager to imply that you have been activated all along by a simple emotional attachment for a man—even if he is a gallant swashbuckling Thief—whom you never saw before? I ask this, not because I expect answers here and now but so that you will understand the necessity, from our point of view, for what must follow."

Keiris finally knew the shape of physical despair. It was

a leaden numbing thing that seized one nerve after the other and made her rotten with fear.

"What do you—they—want to know, Bern?" she said. It was not a question but rather an admission of defeat. Her voice sounded oddly plaintive in her ears.

Haze-Gaunt nodded to Shey, who stepped up and swiftly strapped a disc-like thing to her arm—a portable verigraph. The needles that circulated veinous blood through the instrument stung sharply; then the pain was gone. The thing's eye blinked green at each heartbeat. She rubbed her arm above the instrument.

They would make her own body betray her. They would program it with their insidious drugs, and then they would feed questions to it, just as though they were talking to a computer, and the answers would flash out as colors on that incorruptible little crystal, just like lines slavishly jumping out on a CRT. Green for truth, red for lies. Destroyed by a needle prick. She couldn't even claim they had broken her under torture. It was bitterly unfair. She suppressed a whimper.

Haze-Gaunt waited a moment for the scopolamine to take effect. Then he asked, "Had you ever known Alar before tonight?"

"No," she replied with what she believed perfect truth.

To her utter amazement and wondering surmise, the blinking green eye of the instrument turned slowly red.

"You have seen him before," observed Haze-Gaunt grimly. "You should know better than to try to deceive the verigraph on the first question. You know well enough that it is effective over a three-minute period."

She sat down dizzily. The instrument had said she had lied—had said that she really *had* known Alar before. But where? When?

"Perhaps a glimpse somewhere," she murmured faintly. "I can't account for it otherwise."

"Have you carried information to the Thieves before?"

"I don't know." The light flashed a vivid yellow.

"She isn't sure," interpreted Shey smoothly, "but she thinks she has occasionally betrayed information in the past, evidently through anonymous intermediaries, and she believes it reached the Thieves. We have only two minutes before the 'graph becomes ineffective. Let's hurry on."

"In these matters," Thurmond asked her harshly, "do you act independently?"

"Yes," she whispered.

The light immediately flashed red.

"A categorical lie," sniggered Shey. "She's working for someone. Who directs you?" he demanded.

"No one."

Again the red light.

"Is it a cabinet member?" demanded Thurmond.

Even in her near-stupor she marveled at his eternal suspicion of treachery in high places.

"No," she whispered.

"But someone in the palace?"

"The palace?"

"Yes, here in the chancellory palace?"

The light was blinking green steadily. She groaned with relief. The Meganet Mind was quartered within the imperial palace, not the chancellory palace.

"The imperial palace, then?" suggested Shey.

She didn't answer but knew the light was burning crimson.

The three men exchanged glances.

"The Imperatrix?" asked Thurmond.

The light turned green. The police minister shrugged his shoulders.

She realized dully that she must faint, but that she could not.

And it came. Haze-Gaunt displayed once again the flash of dazzling intuition that had brought him to the leadership of his wolf pack. He asked:

"Do you receive orders from the Meganet Mind?"

"No."

It was no use. She knew without looking at the light that it must surely have betrayed her.

Oddly, she felt only relief. They had got it out of her without pain. She couldn't blame herself.

Then "Barbellion?" asked Thurmond dubiously, naming the Colonel of the Imperial Guards.

She froze. The three minutes had passed. The verigraph was no longer registering. The light must not have turned red on the name "The Meganet Mind."

"We've run over the time a little," interposed Haze-Gaunt, frowning. "Her blood is buffered again, and her reactions for the last questions were meaningless. We'll have to wait six or seven days for another try at the truth."

"We can't wait," objected Thurmond. "You know we can't wait."

Shey stepped up and disconnected the verigraph. Keiris felt the stab of another needle, and her head was horridly clear again by the time she realized what Haze-Gaunt had replied.

"She's yours, Shey."

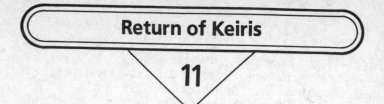

DEAR, DEAR KEIRIS," smiled Shey. "Our rendezvous here was as inevitable as death itself."

From where she lay, strapped to the operating table, the woman sucked in her breath and looked with wide eyes about the room. There was nothing there but the gleaming whiteness, the pans of strange instruments—and Shey, swathed in a white surgical gown.

The psychologist was speaking again, his words interspersed with giggles.

"Do you understand the nature of pain?" he asked, leaning over her as far as his rotundity would permit. "Did you know that pain is the finest of the senses? So few people do. In the gross animality of most of mankind pain is used solely as a notice of physical injury.

"The subtler overtones are missed entirely. Only a few of the enlightened—such as the Hindu fakirs, the Penitentes, the Flagellants—appreciate the supreme pleasures that may be obtained from our sadly neglected proprioceptive system.

"Look!" He pulled back his sleeve deftly, exposed a pulpy raw spot on his inner arm. "I peeled off the epidermis and let flaming drops of ethanol fall there for fifteen minutes, while I sat in my box at the opera, enthralled by the Imperial Ballet's rendition of *Inferno*. In the whole audience

I alone completely appreciated it." He paused and sighed. "Well then, let us begin. You can talk any time you wish. I hope not too soon."

He wheeled up a dial-clustered box and unreeled two needle-tipped wires from it. One needle he jabbed into the palm of her right hand, then strapped it down to the palm with adhesive tape. The other was similarly applied to her right bicep.

"We start with the elementary, and advance to the complex," explained Shey. "You will appreciate the stimuli more fully if you understand their effect. Observe the oscillograph." He pointed to a circular glass panel of dull white, split horizontally by a luminous line.

She cried out involuntarily as a sharp pain shot up her arm—and stayed there, throbbing rhythmically.

Shey giggled. "Nice appetizer, eh? See the cathode beam? It shows that impulses travel up that particular nerve trunk in several speeds. There's the sudden flashing pain— the peak on the cathode tube, traveling about thirty meters a second. Then several slower impulses come up, with speeds down to half a meter a second. They make up the dull ache that follows stubbing your toe, or burning your finger.

"These impulses are gathered into larger and larger nerve fibers that eventually pass into the spinal cord and are carried to the thalamus, which sorts out the various stimuli of pain, cold, warmth, touch, and so on, and routes the messages to the cerebrum for action.

"The post central convolution lying just behind the fissure of Rolando seems to get all the pain impulses." He looked up cheerfully and adjusted the needle in her upper arm. "Bored with that monotonous old stimulus? Here's another."

She braced herself but the pain was not nearly so sharp.

"Not much, eh?" said the psychologist. "Just barely above threshold. After stimulation the fiber can't be stimulated again for four-tenths of a millisecond. Then for fifteen milliseconds it goes the other way—hypersensitive—and then it's subnormal again for eighty milliseconds, then normal from then on. It's that fifteen millisecond hypersensitive period that I find so useful—"

Keiris screamed.

"Splendid!" crowed Shey, shutting off the switch on the black box. "And that was on only one nerve in one arm. It's perfectly fascinating to add one pair of electrodes after another until the arms are covered with them, even though the subject generally dies." He turned to the box again.

Somewhere in the room a radiochron was ticking out the seconds with mocking languor.

Alar stared in slow wonder at the bearded starveling in the mirror.

What hour?

What day?

A sharp glance at the chronocal told his incredulous eyes that six weeks had passed since he had locked himself in the study here beneath Lunar Station, in a frantic race against the moment when the combined might of the Thieves and the Imperials would search him out and kill him.

Had he really succeeded in solving the mystery of the star plate?

He didn't know.

He thought he had discovered the identity of that luminous wheel in the lower right hand corner of the negative. He had discovered some very interesting aberrations in the nebulae in the intervening space and had considered several explanations, none of which were entirely satisfactory. He wondered if the Mind knew the answer. He rather suspected he did.

Everyone seemed to know all the answers except him. There was almost a comical injustice in that he, the possessor of the miraculous ear and eye, who had skirted the fringe of godhood that night in Shey's evil chamber, knew so little of himself.

And now this strange and wonderful star plate—it held something that the Mind wanted him to know. But what?

He scratched absently at his beard while his eyes toured the study. From the ceiling lamp dangled a small three-dimensional model of the galaxy. It seemed to apologize for the preposterous scenery beneath, which consisted of—books, gigantic, minuscule, gaudy, modest, in all the tongues of distant Earth.

They swarmed over floor, chairs and tables, half-way up the four walls, a rugged landscape drained here and there by valleys made by Alar as he walked the floor during the past weeks. The valleys were carpeted by a forlorn detritus of discarded scribblings.

In a glaciated cirque of the book-Matterhorn that arched over his work-desk, his electron microscope was enshrined, surrounded by a gray talus of negatives.

His roving eye next caught the glint of the tube of depilatory peeking at him from between the pages of Muir's *Space Mechanics*. A moment later he was again before the mirror, rubbing his beard away by degrees, followed by curious inspection, as men invariably do when they depilate after a long absence from civilization.

But when the stubble was all gone he was appalled at the pinched pallor of his face. He tried to remember when he had last slept or eaten. He couldn't place either event precisely. He vaguely recalled devouring frozen cubes of vegetable soup with his bare fingers.

He walked to the porthole and looked out into the blackness toward a ridge of wild lunar mountains, silver-tinged by the setting sun. Crescented Terra hung in gigantic splendor just above the ridge. He would like to be there now, asking questions of the Mind, of Haven—of Keiris. How long would it be before Earth would again be safe for him? Probably never, with both Thief and Imperial searching. It was a miracle that his imposture here at the observatory had not been detected.

He reflected. Am I here for a purpose? Do I have a destiny? For good? For evil? Shall I share the doom of that wretched Earth? Or can I change those hapless creatures? Ridiculous thought! As John Haven once pointed out, someone would have to go back into the time of dawn man and work an impossibly intricate bit of genetic engineering on their genes and chromosomes. The Neandertals and others before and after them would have to be changed from unreasoning killers to men willing to recognize the brotherhood of men. Toynbee Twenty-two. And forget it.

He shook his head gloomily. What he needed was a brisk walk along the sparse streets of Selena—the lunar settlement that housed the observatory staff and their families. He strode toward his shower room.

Alar had been wandering through the streets about an hour when he saw Keiris.

She was standing alone on the steps of the Geographical Museum, regarding him gravely. A light cape was thrown about her shoulders and she appeared to hold it together with the fingers of her right hand, or possibly a barely visible metal clasp.

The lamps on the museum porticoes threw an unearthly blue light over her bloodless face. Her translucent cheeks were drawn and lined, and her body seemed very thin. There was now a streak of white in her hair, which was knotted unobtrusively at the side of her neck.

To Alar she was completely lovely. For a long time he could only stare, drinking in the moody, ethereal beauty of the composition of light and blue shadow. His torturing frustration was forgotten.

"Keiris!" he whispered. "*Keiris!*"

He walked quickly across the street and she descended the steps stiffly to meet him.

But when he held out both hands to her, she merely lowered her head and seemed to swirl her cape closer. Somehow, he had not expected so cool a reception. They walked silently up the street.

After a moment he asked, "Did Haze-Gaunt give you any trouble?"

"A little. They asked some questions. I told them nothing." Her voice was strangely husky.

"Your hair—have you been ill?"

"I have been in a hospital for the past six weeks," she replied evasively.

"I'm sorry." After a moment he asked, "Why are you here?"

"A friend of yours brought me. A Dr. Haven. He's waiting in your study, now."

Alar's heart leapt. "Has the Society reinstated me?" he asked quickly.

"Not that I know of."

He sighed. "Very well, then. But how did you meet John?"

Keiris studied the dim-lit flaggings of the street. "He bought me in the slave market," she said quietly.

Alar sensed the outline of something ominous. What could have angered Haze-Gaunt to the point of selling her? And why had the Society bought her? He couldn't talk to her about it. Perhaps Haven would know.

"There's really nothing mysterious about it," she continued. "Haze-Gaunt gave me to Shey. When Shey thought I was dead he had me sold to what he thought was a charnel-house buyer, only it turned out to be a surgeon sent by the Thieves. They kept me in their secret hospital for six weeks and as you can see I didn't die. And when Dr. Haven came I told him where you were. We slipped through the blockade last night."

"Blockade?"

"Haze-Gaunt grounded every planetary and spacejet immediately after you left. The Imperials are still combing the hemisphere for you."

He stole a cautious look behind them. "But how could a Thief ship enter Lunar Station? The place is swarming with I.P.'s. You've been spotted, surely. It was insane of

Haven to come. The only reason both of you weren't arrested when you landed was that the I.P.'s hoped you'd lead them to me. Well, we're being tailed right now."

"I know but it doesn't matter." Her voice was quiet, with a soft huskiness. "The Mind told me to come to you. As for Dr. Haven, I question none of his acts. As for you, you'll be safe for several hours.

"Suppose the guards at the landing locker *did* identify Dr. Haven and me, and suppose that I *have* called their attention to you and suppose we *are* being followed. If we don't try to leave Selena they won't do anything, at least not until Thurmond arrives and perhaps Shey. Why should they? They think you can't escape."

He started to make a sarcastic retort, then changed his mind. "Does Haven really think he can get me off the moon?" he queried.

"A high government official, a secret Thief, will plant his bribed guard at the exit port at a certain hour and all of us can escape then." She compressed her lips, gave him a strange side look, and then said without expression: "You won't die on the moon."

"Another prediction of the Meganet Mind, eh? Incidentally, Keiris, who *is* the Mind? Why do you think you have to do everything he says?"

"I don't know who he is. It's said he was once a common circus performer who could answer any question if the answer had ever appeared in print. Then about ten years ago he was in a fire that left his face and hands disfigured.

"After that he couldn't make any more public appearances, and became a clerk in the data banks of the Imperial Science Library. That's where he learned to absorb a two thousand page book in less than a minute and that's where Shey discovered him."

"Go on." He felt a twinge of guilt at pressing her for details about a life she must long to forget. But he had to know.

"About that time Kim disappeared and Haze-Gaunt—took me. I got a note in Kim's handwriting asking me to do whatever the Mind requested. So—"

"Kim?" Something sagged within the Thief.

The woman said quietly: "Kennicot Muir was my husband. You didn't know?"

A great deal was suddenly incisively, painfully clear.

"Keiris Muir," he muttered. "Of course! The wife of the most fabulous, most elusive man in the system. In ten years he hasn't appeared in person to the Society he founded or to the woman he married." He said abruptly, "What makes you think he's alive?"

"Sometimes I wonder myself," she admitted slowly. "It's just that on *that* night, when he left me to go to his fatal interview with Haze-Gaunt, he told me he'd get through and come back for me. A week later, when Haze-Gaunt had installed me in his personal quarters, I received a note in Kim's handwriting asking me not to commit suicide. So I didn't.

"The next month I got another note telling me about the Meganet Mind. About once a year since then there have been other notes in what looks like his handwriting, telling me that he looks forward to the day we can be together again."

"Have you considered that they might be forgeries?"

"Yes, they might be. He may be dead. Perhaps I am naïve for thinking him alive."

"Is that the only evidence you have?—those notes in his handwriting?"

"That's all." Keiris nodded solemnly. "And yet, I think it's significant that none of the wolf pack thinks he's dead, either."

"That includes Haze-Gaunt?"

"Oh yes, Haze-Gaunt is almost certain Kim is in hiding, perhaps overseas."

To Alar that was the strongest possible indication that Muir was indeed alive. The hard, practical chancellor would be certain to hide his secret fears if he thought them baseless.

"But," Alar said, "what about the Mind? What is his connection with the Society?"

"A secret agent, I suppose. His access to the Imperial Science Library is probably of considerable value to the Society."

Alar smiled humorlessly. Keiris's intimacy with greatness had apparently blinded her to the probability that the Society was a mere catspaw of the Mind. You, I, all of us, he thought, caught in the omnivorous meshes of that mysterious net. Ah, Mind with the Meganet, you are well named!

And the comparison led to a startling possibility.

"You say," he began slowly, studying her closely, "that Kennicot Muir disappeared about the same time that the Mind put in his appearance. Does that seem significant to you?"

Her eyes widened, but she didn't say anything.

"Have you considered," he persisted, "that the Meganet Mind might be your husband?"

She was silent for a moment before she replied.

"Yes, I've considered it." Her dark eyes searched his face eagerly. "Have you learned something?"

"Nothing specific." He saw the sudden disappointment reflected in her eyes. "But there seems to be an inordinate number of coincidences connected with the two men."

"The only resemblance between them is in their over-all size. Otherwise they're utterly different."

"The Mind is disfigured, so that would be a perfect disguise. More important is the rise to prominence of the Mind after your husband's disappearance. Note his influence with the Society." Alar watched her carefully. "And he treats you like a special ward."

"They can't be the same man," she said without conviction. There was doubt, now, in her eyes.

"What proof do you have that they *aren't?*" Alar said gently.

"Proof?" She obviously had no answer to his question.

"You said," he continued, pursuing the point which formed the basis for her doubt, "that you've weighed the possibility. What made you discard it?"

"I don't know," she replied, beginning to be upset as she felt her confidence fading away. "I just did." She shook her head almost desperately. "I have no proof, if that's what you mean."

He was being cruel, he knew, with his questioning. She wanted to be objective, to face the situation, but the pain within could not be controlled. He hunted frantically through his brain for a final question to settle the doubts in both their minds.

Suddenly he had it. "Has Haze-Gaunt also considered the possibility?"

"Why, yes! Yes, he has!" Her eyes were very wide now.

"To what effect?"

"He rejected the idea completely! I know he did!"

"So!" Alar said and sighed. That was importantly significant—that was negative proof as good as one might expect to find. The interrogation was over. He looked abruptly at the luminous dial on his wrist radio.

"It's four now. If Thurmond left immediately—and we must assume he did—he'll be here with troops by midnight. We have eight hours to complete the solution to the star plate and to blast off. Our first step is the Galactarium, then back to my study and John Haven."

T HE WIZENED CURATOR unlocked the door, and Alar led the woman into the great dark chamber of the Galactarium. The door closed quietly behind them, and their eyes strained forward in the cold gloom, sensing rather than seeing the vastness of the place.

"A gallery circles the interior," whispered Alar. "We'll take a moving platform to the necessary point."

He led her down the ramp and they were soon speeding around the dark periphery of the great room.

Within a few seconds the platform slowed to a stop in front of a vaguely lit control-board. Keiris smothered a gasp as Alar's hand flew to his saber pommel.

A tall somber figure stood by the panel station. "Good evening, Mrs. Muir, Alar!"

The Thief felt his stomach turn over slowly.

The tall man's laughter welled in ghastly echoes out into the blackness, circling and sodden. His face was that of Gaines, Undersecretary of Spaceways. The voice was that of the Thief judge who had condemned him to death.

Alar was silent, wary, speculative.

The man seemed to read his thoughts. "Paradoxically, Alar, your escape from us was the only thing that could have reinstated you in the Society. It confirmed your ultrahumanity as no number of words could have done. As for me, if you're wondering, I arrived on the sun-bound *Phobos* last night, and I am here now to provide for your safe passage home and to ask if you have discovered the secret of the star plate. Our time is growing very short."

"Why do you want to know?" queried Alar.

"I don't, particularly. The important thing is that *you* know."

"That's easily answered, then. I don't know—or at least I don't know the whole story." Alar had a stubborn impulse to maintain a strict silence until he learned more about his role in this fantastic drama. Still, for ill-defined reasons, he trusted this man who had once wanted his life. "Look out there," he said simply, pointing into the man-made space before them.

The three of them stared into the silent vastness while Alar flicked a switch on the panel. Even Gaines seemed subdued.

Sol with his ten planets sprang into glowing three-dimensional view before them. Cerberus, the newly discovered trans-Plutonian planet, was nearly a mile away, barely visible. Expertly the Thief manipulated the dials and the system began rapidly to shrink. The three picked up opera glasses from the panel pockets and watched. Finally, Alar spoke.

"Our sun is now about the size of a very small speck of luminous dust, and even with our magnifiers we can't see Jupiter." He quickly began to activate more switches. "That's Alpha Centauri, a visual binary, over two hundred yards away from the sun on the present scale. The bright one on the other side is Sirius. And there's Procyon. They're accompanied by dwarfs too faint to see.

"Within this mile-diameter Galactarium there are now about eighty of the stars nearest the sun. On this scale the galaxy would fit in a space about as big as the moon. So we'll have to shrink the projections still more to see any substantial part of the galaxy."

He turned more dials and a great glowing wheel with spiraling spokes began to form before them. "*The* galaxy— our local universe," he said softly. "Or at least ninety-five percent of it, scaled down to a mile across and one-tenth of a mile thick. It's just a haze of light now—the Milky Way.

"The main identifying features are the two Magellanic Clouds. For more accurate identification we can refer to the positions of the spiral arms, the hundred globular clusters and the configuration of the star cloud in the center of the galaxy. Now watch."

The wheel and its Magellanic satellites shrank quickly. "The Galactarium is now on a diametric scale of five million light years. Far off to the right, about seven hundred and fifty thousand scale light years away, is our sister galaxy, M thirty-one in Andromeda, with her own satellite clusters M thirty-two and NGC two hundred and five. Below are two smaller galaxies, IC one thousand six hundred and thirteen and M thirty-three. On the other side is NGC six thousand eight hundred and twenty-two. The universe-fragment you now see," he concluded simply, "is exactly what I found on the star plate."

"But this is old stuff," protested Gaines in heavy disappointment.

"No," interjected Keiris. "Alar means that he has seen our own galaxy *from outside.*"

"That's right," said the Thief. "For two centuries astronomic theory has predicted that our own galaxy would be visible as soon as a telescope were constructed capable of penetrating the thirty-six-billion-light-year diameter of the universe."

"So!" Gaines said. "From the outside!" He beat a faint tattoo with his opera glasses against the panel pocket. "Then we're peering clear across the universe!" He seemed immensely impressed.

"Well," Alar said, giving a fleeting wry smile, "that's not very much to my credit. When the Lunar Observatory was finished it was just a question of time before my discovery was made. So my contribution in *that* direction is largely routine."

Keiris glanced sharply at him.

"Have you discovered something else, then?" she asked.

"Yes. In the first place, light from the Milky Way, passing in a closed circuit across the universe, should return only after thirty-six billion years, so that what we now see on the plate should be our galaxy as of thirty-six billion years ago, on the very eve of its formation from cosmic dust. Instead, the plate shows the Milky Way as of now—today—just as you see it out there."

"But that's impossible!" exclaimed Gaines. "There ought to be a thirty-six-billion-year lag!"

Smiling, the Thief said, "It should be impossible, shouldn't it? But the positions of the galactic spiral arms, the peripheral velocity of the nebula as a whole, the positions of the globular clusters, the spectral age of our own sun, even the positions of the planets, including Terra, prove otherwise."

"Then how do you explain it?" asked Keiris.

"Here is my hypothesis: According to Einstein, time multiplied by the square root of minus one is equated to Euclidean space. That is, a light year of distance equals a year of time multiplied by the square root of minus one. So if space is finite, so must time be. And like space, time curves and bends back on itself, so that there is no beginning and no end.

"Our galaxy moves simultaneously along time and space coördinates like this." He held up two pencils crossed at right angles. "Let the x-axis be time, the y-axis space, our galaxy located at the intersection. Now I move the y-pencil to the right, and simultaneously push it up. Anything at the intersection will be moving in both coördinates."

He offered the two pencils to Keiris, but with a toss of her head she deferred the honor to Gaines. The Undersecretary took the two slim implements and, holding them together at right angles, moved them back and forth and up and down. His lips were pursed and his eyes were intent. Keiris was concentrating on the demonstration, too.

Alar watched the two of them adjusting themselves to the concept. He leaned towards them and touched the pencils.

"Now," he said, "suppose you substitute two hoops for the pencils, so that the hoop frames intersect each other at right angles like the frame of a toy gyroscope. Let one hoop be equivalent to thirty-six billion light years of space and the other equivalent to thirty-six billion years of time, with our galaxy always at their intersection.

"I'll assume further that for any given time-space intersection there can be but one distribution of matter, with the corollary that, when the same intersection recurs, the same matter will be there. So, after the hoops have made one-half revolution, the intersection does recur, and it follows that our galaxy is in two places at once, or to be more precise, in the same space at the same time.

"But space and time have vanished and rematerialized across the poles of the universe and, when they did, our galaxy materialized with them. The joker in my illustration is that we are tempted to view the rotation of the hoops in Euclidean space, while they're really associated only through the square root of minus one via the fourth dimension. Only their intersections—just two geometric points—have mutual Euclidean values."

He took back the two pencils Gaines was offering.

"And, since the two intersections are diametrically opposite in the space-time cycle, one should always be thirty-six billion years ahead of the other, so that when light starts from the 'future' intersection and travels across the poles of time and space to the lagging intersection, it arrives at the other thirty-six billion years later, to be received by the same space-time-matter continuum from which it originated. That's why the 'mirror' galaxy was the same age as ours now is, when its light began that long journey."

The three were silent a moment. Finally Gaines said, almost diffidently, "What do you think it means, Alar?"

"Standing by itself, it means nothing. But viewed in the light of another peculiarity appearing on the plate it might mean a great deal. For example, it seems to suggest the possibility of traveling backward in time. We can talk about it after I've seen John Haven and asked him some questions."

Alar dropped his opera glasses back into the pocket and moved close to the control panel. He spun the dials back to neutral, flipped the power switch. The light points in the huge room dwindled rapidly into nothingness. For a moment the three of them stood there silently in the heavy darkness which had come with the disappearance of the starry projection. "We'd better leave now," he said.

As their eyes grew accustomed to the faint wall lights which had reappeared, Alar stepped on the moving platform, Keiris and Gaines moving in step behind him.

The platform carried them quietly around the great curving edge of the room to the ramp. They started up the ramp toward the entrance hall beyond the gallery. Near the top, Alar suddenly halted.

"A guard," he said. He could see an I.P. officer standing near a huge steel column, hands on hips, talking in a low voice to a second man.

Keiris was huddled against Alar's back, Gaines at his side, a firm left hand on his shoulder.

"We should have nothing to fear," Gaines said. But the tone of his voice was not quite so positive.

"It will be best if we're cautious," Alar replied. He studied the thin, shriveled figure of the second man. It was the curator. "You wait here. I'll check out with the curator and inform him we'll leave by the side exit." He pointed to the deeper shadows to his left, where a dim red bulb was barely visible. "I'll meet you there."

Before Keiris or Gaines could reply, Alar stalked off toward the two figures.

Keiris watched him approach the others, anxiety drawing lines on her face. The I.P. officer stepped back a pace, then followed the curator and Alar as they wandered toward the Galactarium office, conversing as they went.

"Come," Gaines whispered and led her toward the red light.

The minute that it took Alar to rejoin them seemed like an hour to her. Her fears were completely swept away when he paced up to her, relaxed and confident.

"Everything all right?" Gaines asked hoarsely.

"We're in no immediate danger, I'm certain," Alar replied. He caught the swift look from Gaines. "Let's go away from here first and I'll explain further."

They pushed open the exit, stepped outside. The door swung shut behind them, locking itself. They stood for a second on the side passageway, facing the main corridor fifty feet away.

"The I.P. asked me to identify myself," the Thief said. "I gave him my credentials as Dr. Philip Ames and he was satisfied. Then he asked me where the rest of the party was."

Gaines frowned, continuing to peer down the passageway toward the main corridor.

"I explained that I just left you two in the gallery. He asked me, then, what your names were."

Keiris sucked her breath in sharply. Gaines turned his head and asked softly, "What did you say?"

Alar smiled slightly. "I told him the truth."

"You did?" Gaines said incredulously.

"It was the best way. If the I.P. really knew my true identity, nothing would be served by lying. And if he didn't, then the truth would allay his suspicions."

"But he'll report our get-together to his superiors," Gaines pointed out. "No one knows we've just arrived on the moon. In a couple of hours there'll be I.P.'s swarming all over us."

"I'm afraid," Alar said ominously, "that they already know. The nonchalance of that I.P. at the mention of your names gave it away to me."

After a moment of shocked silence, Gaines said, "I suppose it was too much to expect to hide our arrival. We'll just have to keep out of sight and not provoke them and hope that they'll wait until they get direct orders from Thurmond." Gaines was frowning again. "What do you think, Alar? Should we dodge around a bit in the back passageways or split up?"

The Thief reflected for a moment. The three of them together would find it more difficult to escape from trouble if it arose, but if they stayed together they would stand a better chance to avoid it.

"Let's take a back way," Alar said. He looked at Keiris, whose eyes had widened in alarm and whose body seemed to have shrunk within her swirling cloak. He glanced at the streak of white which ran across her head and into the knotted bun at the side of her slender neck. She still looked ill. He wished she could be spared all the tension that was being forced into her life. He patted her shoulder briefly. "Don't worry, Keiris. They don't have us on the run—we're just playing it safe."

Gaines stalked off, away from the main corridor, without a backward look. As Alar and Keiris started to follow, she exchanged a penetrating glance with him. Her look was so full of tenderness and concern for him—and he involuntarily returned it so forcefully—that he was for the moment emotionally shaken.

Then she was ahead of him, close behind Gaines.

They weaved through corridors, criss-crossing the main ones, for nearly half an hour.

"I'll try to answer your last question first, my boy," said John Haven. The biologist studied his protégé warmly as he lit his pipe and took a few experimental puffs. Finally he settled back in his chair. "Do you know what 'ecstasy' means?"

Keiris and Gaines were following avidly.

"You may assume that I know the dictionary definition, John," answered Alar, absorbing the older man with keen eyes.

"That isn't enough. Oh, it tells you it's from the Greek

verb 'existani,' meaning 'to put out of place.' But out of place from what? Into what? What is this peculiar mental state known as 'ecstasy'? All we know is, that it may be attained through alcohol, drugs, savage dancing, music, and in various other ways.

"During your encounter with Shey, in your moment of greatest need, you probably passed into—or beyond—the state we are discussing. In so doing you burst from your old three-dimensional shell and found yourself in what was apparently a new world.

"Actually, if I have followed your description accurately, it was simply an aspect of your eternal four-dimensional body, which has three linear dimensions and one 'time' dimension. The ordinary human being sees only three dimensions—the fourth time, he senses intuitively as an extra dimension.

"But when he tries to imagine the shape of a thing extending through the time dimension, he finds that he has simply lost a space dimension. He imagines his body extending through time just as your body did during your experience. In this new world the three dimensions visible to you were two linear and one of time, which combined to give an appearance of regular three-dimensional solidity."

"You are saying," said Alar slowly and thoughtfully, "that I viewed my four-dimensional body through three new dimensions."

"Not three *new* dimensions. They were all old. Height and breadth were the same. The only apparently new dimension was time, substituting for depth. The cross section of your body simply extended with changing time until it became an endless pillar.

"And you stepped out of your pillar when the pain became unbearable. The difference in your ecstasy and that of the Greeks was that you didn't have to go back into time at the same moment—or place—that you left."

"John," said Alar with gloomy, almost exasperated surmise, "do you realize that I could have stepped back into time at a period prior to my amnesia? That I could have solved my personal mystery with utter ease? And now—I don't know how to get back, except perhaps through that unutterable hell of pain." His chest lifted in vast regret. "Well, then, John? About my other question—who am I?"

Haven looked toward Gaines.

"I think I'd better try to answer that one," interposed the Undersecretary. "But there isn't any answer, really. When you crawled up on the river bank five years ago you were clutching something in your hand—this." He gave Alar a small leather-bound book.

The Thief studied it curiously. It was water-stained, and the cover and pages had shriveled and warped during drying. The cover was stamped in gold:

T-22, Log.

He was breathing considerably faster when he sought Gaines's eyes. But the Undersecretary simply said, "Look inside."

Alar folded back the cover and read the first entry:

" 'July 21, 2177 . . .' "

His eyes narrowed. "That's next week. There's an error in the date."

"Finish the entry," urged Haven.

"July 21, 2177. This will be my only statement, since I know where I am going and when I shall return. There is little now to be said and, as perhaps the last living human being, I have no inclination to say it. Within a few minutes the T-22 will be traveling faster than light. Under more cheerful circumstances I should be exceedingly interested in following the incredible evolution that has already started in my companion."

That was all.

"The rest of the book is blank," said Haven shortly.

Alar ran nerveless fingers through his hair. "Are you saying that I'm the man who wrote that? That I was on the ship?"

"You may or may not have been on the ship. But we are certain you didn't make the log entry."

"Who did?"

"Kennicot Muir," said Gaines. "His handwriting is unmistakable."

Visitor from the Stars

13

ALAR'S EYES OPENED a trifle wider and fastened hawklike on the Space Undersecretary. "How," he asked, "can you be so sure I'm not Kennicot Muir?"

"He was a larger man. Furthermore, the fingerprints, eye capillaries, pupil chroma, blood type, age and dental and skeletal characteristics are different. We've considered the point very carefully, hoping to find points of identity. There aren't any. Whoever you are, you're not Kennicot Muir."

"And yet," Alar said, with a grimace which was almost a grin, "is that necessarily conclusive evidence?"

"Why—what do you mean?" Gaines was honestly puzzled. Haven's eyes had been almost completely closed in thought, now he opened them wide.

"It would appear," Alar said, "that the trip might have caused some very peculiar changes. Isn't it possible that, as Muir, my body was distorted? Enough so that I am a completely disguised Kennicot Muir? Disguised so well that I can't even recognize myself?"

Gaines' mouth opened and closed several times before he replied: "I think it's impossible."

"Perhaps not impossible," Haven said slowly, "but improbable, shall we say. As a theory, there is nothing to support it except that a lot of our puzzling questions could be glibly answered by it."

"Well, then," Alar continued, turning first from Gaines to Haven and then back to Gaines. "What about the Meganet Mind?"

"The Mind?" Gaines repeated, rubbing his chin. "You think Muir might be the Mind?"

"Yes, I think it's possible."

Gaines chuckled. "It would be a very, very fascinating development if it were true. Unfortunately it isn't. The only resemblance between the Mind and Muir is in the over-all size of their bodies. There have been investigations several times—that possibility has been discarded."

"Investigators can be bribed," Alar said. He stretched his fingers over the front ends of the arm rests of his chair, shifting his glance briefly to them and then back to the two older men. "Records can be destroyed or forged. Facts can be hidden."

"That may be true," Gaines said flatly. "But I know personally that the Meganet Mind existed long before Muir ever disappeared. Not as the Mind, *per se*, of course, but even then showing the potential of what he would eventually become."

Haven made a clicking noise with his pipe stem against his teeth. "The chances of you, Alar, being Muir," he said thoughtfully, "as small as they are, are still better than that of the Mind being Muir."

During this time Keiris had not taken her eyes from Alar's face.

The Thief sighed. "Well, then, that's that. But what about the date of the entry? July twenty-first, two thousand one hundred and seventy-seven is only a few days off. Since the book is at least five years old Muir must have made a blunder in the date."

"We don't know the answer," admitted Gaines. "We thought you might."

The Thief smiled humorlessly. He said:

"How could Muir return in the *T-twenty-two* before it was even built?"

The room slowly grew quiet. Nothing was audible except Keiris's suppressed jerky breathing. Alar felt a nerve throbbing restlessly in the small of his back. Haven pulled placidly at his pipe but his eyes missed nothing.

"The non-Aristotelians at their wildest never suggested that time could be traversed negatively unless—" Alar rubbed the side of his cheek in deep thought. The others waited.

"You said the pilot panel of the crashed ship indicated the possibility of speeds beyond the velocity of light?" he asked Gaines.

"So it seemed. The drive proved to be virtually identical with that designed for the *T-twenty-two*."

"But by elementary Einsteinian mechanics transphotic velocities are impossible," remonstrated Alar. "Nothing can exceed the speed of light—theoretically, at least. The fact that I may have been aboard a ship similar to the *T-twenty-two* means nothing to me. In fact the very name *T-twenty-two* seems meaningless. Where did our *T-twenty-two* get its name?"

"Haze-Gaunt adopted the name on a suggestion from the Toynbeean Institute," replied Gaines. "It is simply an abbreviation of 'Toynbeean Civilization Number Twenty-two.' The great historian gave each civilization an index number. The Egyptaic was Number One, the Andean Number Two, the Sinic Number Three, the Minoan Number Four, and so on. Our present civilization, the Western, is Toynbee Number Twenty-one.

"The Toynbeeans secretly theorized that an interstellar ship might save Toynbee Twenty-one by launching us into a new culture—Toynbee Twenty-two—in the same way the sail launched the Minoan thalassocracy, the horse the nomadic cultures, and the stone road the Roman Empire. So *T-twenty-two* is more than just the name of a ship. It may prove the life-bridge, linking two destinies."

Alar nodded. "Quite plausible. There's no harm in hoping." But his thoughts were elsewhere. The *Phobos* that had brought Gaines was sunward bound. In the solarions would be men who had known Muir intimately. And then this question of negative time. How could a space-ship land before it took off?

Keiris broke into his revery. "Since we've come to a standstill on solving your identity," she suggested, "suppose you tell us the rest of your star plate discovery. In the Galactarium you said there was more to come."

"Very well, then," agreed Alar. He plunged abruptly into his theme. "Ever since the completion of Lunar Station, we have assumed that it would be just a question of time until we penetrated the whole of space and found our own galaxy at the opposite pole of the universe.

"That was predictable and my discovery simply bore out the prediction. But there were some other developments in that section of the sky that were not so easily predictable.

"Let us go back a bit. Five years ago, as any student of astronomy knows, a body of incalculable mass, apparently originating at a point in space near our own sun cluster, possibly quite near our own solar system, sped outward into space.

"It passed near the M Thirty-one galaxy, disrupted its outer edge with assorted novae and star collisions and then, apparently traveling at a speed greater than light, disappeared about eighteen billion light years out. By 'disappeared' I mean that astronomers were no longer able to detect its influence on galaxies near the line of hypothetical flight.

"The reason they couldn't was that they were no longer looking in the right direction. The body had passed the midpoint of the universe, with respect to its point of origin and had begun to return. Naturally it was approaching in the opposite direction, which is of course the same direction in which the lunar reflector must be collimated to pick up our galaxy.

"In the six weeks that I have studied this sky-sector I have watched the effect of the unknown body on galaxies near its line of return and I have computed its path and velocity, with considerable accuracy. The velocity, incidentally, is decreasing very rapidly from its outer space peak of two billion light years per year.

"Six weeks ago, when I first began my observations, it had almost completed its circuit of the universe and was returning to our own galaxy. Yesterday it passed so close to the Magellanic Clouds that its attraction drew them toward one another in what may be a collision course. In the Lesser Cloud I have already counted twenty-eight novae."

He concluded tersely. "This body will land on Earth on July twenty-first."

A hush fell over the group. The only sound for several minutes was the rasping from Haven's empty pipe.

"The queer thing," mused Gaines, "is its varying mass. The disruption of the stars of our own galaxy in Andromeda is an old story, as Alar said. But the Andromeda star cluster was acted upon by something traveling just below the speed of light and with a mass of some twenty million galaxies concentrated at one point.

"But by the time that body reached the M Thirty-one galaxy some three weeks later, its velocity was many times that of light and its mass was incalculable—possibly bordering on the infinite if such a thing is permissible. I have no doubt but that Alar found the same conditions obtaining for its return—a gradual diminution of velocity and mass until, by the time it reaches Earth, it again has very little mass or velocity, at least none capable of affecting this system. Alar has supplied the final piece in the jigsaw puzzle that has driven astronomers crazy for five years. And now the assembled puzzle is even more incomprehensible than its parts."

"You said this body will 'land' on the earth," said Haven. "You think then—"

"It will prove to be another intergalactic ship."

"But even the biggest lunar or solar freighters don't exceed a mass of ten thousand tons," objected Gaines. "The ship that crashed five years ago was really rather small. Even the largest interstellar ship couldn't possibly have a detectable gravitational effect on a planet, let alone on a whole galaxy."

"Objects traveling at trans-photic velocities—even though such velocities are theoretically impossible—would approach infinite mass," reminded Alar. "And don't forget, the mass of this object increased with increasing velocity. Its mass at rest is probably relatively small. But it needn't be large if its velocity is trans-photic. I suspect that a mere gram weight hurled past the M Thirty-one nebula at a velocity of several million c's would do damage comparable to our own hypothetical intergalactic ship."

"But no intergalactic ships were known in the solar system five years ago," protested Keiris, yawning sleepily. "And you said that it *left* our system five years ago and passed M Thirty-one at many times the velocity of light. Do you mean there are two intergalactic ships? One that arrived five years ago from parts unknown and a second one that left here five years ago and is due to return next week?"

Alar laughed harshly. "Insane, isn't it? Especially when there were no intergalactic or even interstellar ships in existence in the solar system five years ago."

"Maybe the Eastern Federation furnished it," suggested Haven. "I have a suspicion that Haze-Gaunt has consistently underestimated them."

"Not likely," said Gaines. "We know they've got a tremendous plutonium production network, but that's just talcum powder compared to muirium. And they'd have to have muirium for an interstellar drive and they don't have it—yet."

Alar began pacing the floor. Two intergalactic ships. One crashed five years ago and he must have been on it. Another was due to arrive on July 21—next week—bearing whom? Furthermore, on earth, the *T-twenty-two* was due to blast off in the early morning of July 21. Again—with whom?

By the river that bore him, that made *three* ships! He groaned and gnawed at his lip. It seemed that the answer was within his grasp, that it lay on the tip of his tongue. That if he solved this riddle he would know who he was. He knew Haven and Gaines were watching him covertly.

How strange that he, the apprentice, had grown so in stature within the past few weeks. And yet he had no sensation of development. It seemed that the others were growing dull, slow-witted. The genius, he knew, never appears particularly intelligent to himself.

He stopped and looked at the woman.

Keiris seemed to be asleep. Her head had fallen forward on her right shoulder, and her lock of gray hair had dropped over her right eye. Her face had assumed the same waxen pallor that had characterized her since her arrival at the observatory. Her chest rose and fell rhythmically under her enveloping cape.

As he stared at her closed and sunken eyes, the conviction seized him that he had seen her thus before—*dead*.

The Thief blinked. The hallucination was undoubtedly the result of overwork and sleeplessness. With his nervous system thus deranged he could endanger the lives of all of them.

"Gaines," he whispered, "your guard won't relieve the regular I.P. officer at the landing docks for another two hours. Let's all take a nap until then."

"I'll stand watch," volunteered Haven.

Alar smiled. "If they want to kill us, finding out about it in advance won't do us any good. I'll wake us up in plenty of time."

Haven patted a yawn. "All right."

Alar got down on the cold metal tiles just in front of Keiris' chair, forced his mind to become blank, and was instantly asleep.

After a quarter of an hour Keiris listened carefully to the steady breathing of her three companions, then opened her eyes and studied the man asleep at her feet. Her eyes soon came to rest on his upturned face.

It was a strange, unworldly face—yet attractive and gentle. A deep peace lay about the eyes. As she watched him, the lines in her own cheeks softened a little.

She crouched forward slowly, her moody, half-opened eyes fixed on the man's closed ones, and then got out of her chair entirely and stooped beside him.

She stiffened, then relaxed. Across the room Gaines mumbled fitfully and shifted in his chair.

Again she bent over the sleeping Thief until her eyes were but a few inches from his face. After a brooding pause, she eased back into the chair, slipped the sandal from her right foot with the toe of her left and flexed her toes luxuriously over the material of Alar's left sleeve. Her right foot reached hesitantly toward his hand, then quickly withdrew.

She took a deep breath and clenched her teeth, and the next instant her long toes, like fingers, were caressing the man's hand, barely touching the skin. She let her foot rest against the back part, across the knuckles and fingers, so much like an awkward hand gently holding his.

For a while she remained that way. Then she withdrew her foot and knelt forward. Her eyes, once more inches from his own closed ones, studied him. Satisfied that he was deeply asleep, she tilted her head and laid her cheek to his. She could feel the faint stubble of a new beard, the firm, angular cheekbone. Her spine tingled as his uncombed black hair brushed her forehead and pressed against her own. Her face was flushed and hot, and she had a curious feeling that time was standing still.

Toward the end of the second hour Alar quickened his breathing. She drew herself back silently, thrust her foot into the sandal just before he opened his eyes and looked at her.

His eyes roved somberly over her body, which was completely hidden from throat to knees by her cape, then returned to her face. He said quietly, "You have no arms."

She turned her face away.

"I should have guessed. Was it Shey?"

"It was Shey. The Thief surgeons told me there wasn't enough left of them—that they had to amputate to save my life."

"Some remarkable prosthetics are available."

"I know. The thieves fitted me with computerized arms. I could never get used to them. I let them go. But it isn't too bad. I can wash my face, thread a needle, hold a knife—"

"You know that Thieves are not permitted to kill even in self-defense, Keiris?"

"I don't want you to kill Shey. It doesn't matter any more."

The Thief lay on the cold floor, his eyes soft and thoughtful. Then he pushed himself to his knees, reached out, grasped her around the waist gently and lowered her to the pillow beside him. She sat there, silently, feet tucked under, as he curled himself in front of her, close to her.

"Keiris," he said, keeping his hands at her waist. "It matters to me. It matters to me how you feel, whether you can be happy now." His face was near to hers and he caught that exasperatingly familiar scent which came from her. Again he wondered if he had known this still beautiful woman in his phantom past. Several times there had seemed to come from her the faintest hint of recognition.

She just stared at him. Not wild-eyed, but calmly, almost tenderly, as though she too sensed the bond between them and accepted it. The lines in her face had loosened and the increase of moisture in her large black eyes magnified the unfathomable emotion in them. Unrouged to the extent she usually was, yet there was a warm color in her face now.

"I don't know what it is," he said simply, "but I feel a kinship toward you. Something unexplainable." He felt her body tense beneath his hands.

"I know what you feel, my dear," she said. "And neither can I explain it. I have always loved Kim, I always shall love him. But I know that to love you too will not be disloyal." She turned her head sharply away and her hair swung softly against her neck.

Alar thought back into the vanished hours. He recalled how he had met this woman, and how they had gone to the great ball together, and how they had parted there. He relived that final terrible scene in his mind. Aloud, he mused: "You said I reminded you of someone you used to know. It was Kennicot Muir, wasn't it?"

"Yes."

"And yet I am not Muir. There's not the faintest resemblance."

She raised her head. She was not crying, though her eyes were sparklingly wet. "True," she said. "You are completely different from him—and yet I felt when we first met that I once before had seen your face, with those oh so intense dark eyes."

He took his hands from her waist and cupped them around her face.

"Keiris," he said, the name a caress on his lips, "one day, not so long from now, we will know who I am." He put his hands in his lap. "We must not give up until we find that day."

"We won't," she said.

Alar lay his head on her knees, hiding from her the hard concentration in his eyes.

He remained in that twisted position for many minutes, unable to relax.

At last the woman spoke, her cheek briefly stroking his ear. "Gaines's guard is probably on duty by now."

"Yes, I know." He got heavily to his feet and wakened the others.

Gaines rubbed his eyes and stretched. "The three of you will have to stay here a moment until I check out clearance with my man," he warned.

He stepped into the corridor, and the panel wound shut quietly behind him.

Alar was grateful for the delay. Ever since he had learned that the *Phobos* had docked, en route for the sun, he had been making calculations. Even now, despite the trauma wrought within him by what Shey had done to Keiris, his thoughts were sunward.

On the sun would be station masters who had served under Muir. If he could meet just one who knew Muir's whereabouts—just one who could explain why he, Alar, had been found with the Log of the *T-twenty-two* in Muir's handwriting . . .

On the other hand, a quasi-safety awaited him on Terra, under the protection of the Society. There he could pursue his personal mystery in relative peace and quiet. And there he could be with Keiris, who really needed him now.

"Gaines ought to have been back before now," he said

to Haven shortly. "Something may have gone wrong with his plan. I'd better reconnoiter."

Haven shook his head. "No, boy. I'll go."

Apparently Haven still viewed him as nonexpendable. On the other hand he knew from his past experience with danger that he would be more likely to come back alive than Haven.

"You'd better stay with the girl," urged the biologist persuasively.

Against his better judgment Alar let the older man through the panel and watched him as he walked slowly up the corridor. At the first intersection Haven turned left toward the passenger docks. His head jerked once, and, leaning awkwardly against the intersection corner, he tried to turn around. Then he slumped to the floor.

Keiris watched Alar's body grow rigid. "What's wrong?" she whispered tensely.

The Thief turned an ashen face to her. "He has just been killed with a poison dart." Stricken eyes looked into hers and beyond. He had to breathe several times before he could speak again. "You stay here. I'm going out there."

But she followed him closely as he stepped through the panel, and he knew it was futile to insist that she remain. Together they walked slowly up the corridor.

The Thief could not take his eyes from the sprawling body of the man who had walked into death—for him. He could not think but knew he must think, and quickly.

He paused a few feet before the intersection and looked at the face of his dead friend. It was a craggy, noble face, almost beautiful now in its final peace.

While he gazed, the misty stupor that numbed his mind evaporated and he had a plan. He licked his lips and cleared his throat. His scheme required that the killers show themselves, but to lure them out he would have to expose himself in the intersection, with the probability that they would shoot first and ask questions later. It was a risk he had to run.

"I am unarmed," he called. "I wish to surrender."

The military heart, he knew, longed for recognition. The capture of a man who had eluded even the great Thurmond might bring a transfer to Terra and rapid promotion. He hoped an imaginative officer was in charge of the detail.

He stepped into the intersection.

Nothing happened.

Around the corner he could see Gaines's body sprawled out lifeless. A wicked metal sliver protruded from his neck. His bribed guard had evidently been discovered.

"Put your hands up, Alar—slowly," said a tense voice behind him. "You too, sister."

"I will do so, but madame has no arms and cannot raise her hands," said Alar, concealing the rising excitement in his voice. Arms high, he turned slowly and saw a young I.P. officer covering him with a snub-nosed gun, apparently powered by compressed air, or by a mechanically wound spring, to give a muzzle velocity of a hundred or so meters a second—just slow enough to penetrate Thief armor.

"You're right," said the officer grimly, noting Alar's rapid survey of the weapon. "It's not accurate beyond fifty yards, but its poison darts kill faster than bullets. Fourteen of these guns are covering you from peepholes at this instant." He pulled a pair of handcuffs from his pocket and approached the two cautiously.

The icy exterior of the Thief's face concealed a frantically racing mind. Both eyes were focused on the radioreceptor button on the guard's right shoulder, directly below the ear, that connected all guard personnel with the central police room. Alar's eyes were growing beady and feverish but nothing was happening.

He knew he was capable of emitting photic beams in the infra-red with a wave length of at least half a millimeter. The U.H.F. intercom band certainly shouldn't exceed a meter. Yet his eyes were pouring out the electromagnetic spectrum from a few Angstroms to several meters, without raising a squeak in the receptor button.

Something had gone wrong. He was aware of Keiris's body shivering near his side.

In another instant the I.P. would step around to slap the handcuffs on him from behind, and he would lose precious visual contact with the receptor disc.

A bead of perspiration slid down Alar's cheek and dangled at his stubbled chin.

"A.M." said Keiris quietly.

Of course! Amplitude modulation, unheard of since the earliest days of radio, could be used here, where there was virtually no static.

Suddenly the button whistled. The officer stopped uncertainly.

"Instructions for Gate Eleven," intoned the receptor button. "It has been decided to permit the Alar group to 'escape' in their ship. No further attempt shall be made to kill or capture members of the party. End."

Although modified by the liaison neural network that integrated his larynx, optic lobe and retina, further disguised by the imperfections of the one-inch speaker cone on the officer's shoulder, it seemed to Alar that the other could not fail to recognize the voice of the man he was about to manacle.

"You heard Center, mister," said the officer harshly. "Get going. Carry this stiff with you; I'll have the other sent out." His face was knotted in a hard smile. Quite evidently he expected the great lunar guns to open up on the tiny craft immediately after it had blasted off.

The Thief knelt without a word and gently gathered Haven's body into his arms. The body of the older man seemed curiously shriveled and small. Only now did Alar realize what stature the bare fact of being alive contributed to flesh and bone.

Keiris led the way and opened the panels for them. The little spacer was just ahead. To one side of it lay a larger freighter, the *Phobos*. Someone was on the landing platform and calling into the sunbound ship. "No word yet. We'll give him three minutes."

Alar's heart skipped a beat. Slowly he climbed the ramp to the Thief spacer, stooping as he entered.

His lifeless burden he placed on one of the rear bunks.

A puffing guard dragged Gaines in behind him, left the body on the cabin floor and departed without a word.

Alar looked up pensively, and after a few seconds realized that he was gazing into Keiris's somber eyes.

"My hypothesis was wrong," he said.

"You mean about the two—or was it three—intergalactic ships?"

"Yes. I said that one left the earth five years ago, crossed the universe and is due to return in a few days—on July twenty-first."

She waited.

"It can't be returning," said Alar, still seeming to stare through her, "because it hasn't left yet."

The cabin was utterly silent.

"To travel at a velocity greater than light," continued the Thief, "*seems* to require that the Einsteinian equation for the equivalence of mass and energy be overthrown. But the conflict is only apparent. The mass of a Newtonian body may be restated in terms of an Einsteinian body through a correction factor thus—"

He wrote the formula on a bulkhead with a pencil:

$$m \frac{c}{\sqrt{c^2 - v^2}} = M.$$

"Here c is the velocity of light, v the velocity of the moving body, m is Newtonian mass and M is Einsteinian mass. As v increases, of course, M must grow. As v approaches c, M approaches infinity. Heretofore we have considered a limiting velocity. Yet it can't be, because something—my hypothetical intergalactic ship—has crossed the universe in only five years—less than one-billionth the time required by light. So v *can* be greater than c.

"But when v is greater than c, it would seem that Einsteinian mass M must be meaningless, involving as it does the square root of a negative number. But such a conclusion is inconsistent with the observed effect of the ship on galactic matter during the whole of its flight.

"Now the alternative to meaningless M is negative v, which would make v-square positive, and the equation then follows the usual pattern for the determination of M. But v is simply a ratio of distance to time. Distance is a positive scalar quantity, but time can be either positive or negative, depending on whether it stretches into the future or the past."

He looked at her in triumph. "What I'm saying is, that it is a necessary and sufficient condition for trans-photic velocities that the ship move backward in time."

"Then," she said wonderingly, "a ship traveling faster than the speed of light would land before it ever blasted off. So there never were three or even two ships *but only one.* The ship that brought you to earth five years ago—"

"Really is the *T-twenty-two,* which won't be launched until July twenty-first."

The woman leaned dizzily against the curving cabin wall.

Alar continued with bitter amusement. "Do I hop into the *T-twenty-two* next week for a five-year cruise backward in time? Is the original unwitting Alar walking the earth at this moment, planning on the same thing? Will he take the original of that little ape of Haze-Gaunt's as a mascot?" He laughed unsteadily. "Why, it's the damnedest thing I ever—" He broke off abruptly. "I'm not returning to Earth with you."

"I know. I'm sorry."

Alar blinked. "You mean, you knew just now, after I told you."

"No. The *Phobos* is en route to the sun. You think you'll be able to find some of my husband's old friends who can tell you something about yourself. The Meganet Mind said you'd try to go if the opportunity arose."

"He did?"

"He further stated that you'd discover your identity there."

"Ah! The Thief's eyes flamed up. "Why didn't you tell me before?"

The woman studied the floor. "Life in a solarion is dangerous."

His laughter was soft, brittle. "Since when has danger been a determining factor with either of us? What's the real reason for holding back?"

She turned up her quiet eyes to his. "Because when you learn about yourself, the information will be useless. The Mind said that *in the act of dying*, you would remember everything." She studied his face anxiously. "If you want to die, why not return to the Society and do it profitably? Does it really matter who you were five years ago?" Color was flooding into her face.

"I said that we must not give up until we know who I really am," he replied quietly. The Mind's prediction was a shock to him. This was a factor he had never expected.

"But surely," she pleaded, "you don't want to throw your life away to do it?"

"I don't plan to throw it away. You know that."

"Forgive me," she said and shut her eyes tight for a moment as though to control herself. "I must argue with you because of what you said to me back on the floor not so many minutes ago. I thought, perhaps, that my words now might mean something to you."

"But they do, Keiris," he said emphatically.

"But not enough."

Alar sighed. He was at a crossroads now, he knew, and what direction he took no longer concerned him alone. Keiris must be affected by his decision. He regretted nothing he had said to her at that moment when he had allowed the recognition of her mutilation to unseal his lips and reveal his emotions. But by so doing he had given her a claim on him. He was proud of the claim—yet he must bear the consequences.

"Keiris," he said, "I'm not indifferent to your feelings. I would much rather stay with you."

"Then stay."

"You know I can't. I've faced death before. That can't deter me. If I stayed, something important within me would be lost."

"But this time you are forewarned."

"Even if the Mind's prophecy means this specific trip, we can't be certain it will happen. The Mind is not infallible."

"But he is, Alar! He is!"

For the first time within his remembered life Alar found it impossible to make a quick decision. Recovering his past at the cost of his future would be a poor bargain. Perhaps it would be better to return with Keiris and spend a longer, more useful life as a Thief.

He took her by the shoulders. "Goodbye, Keiris."

She turned her head away. "Captain Andrews of the *Phobos* is waiting for Dr. Talbot, of the Toynbeean Institute. Remember Talbot at the ball? He's a Thief and has orders from the Mind to let you go in his place."

Free will!

For a moment it seemed to him that every man in the solar system was just a pawn on the Mind's horizonless chessboard. "You have a stage goatee for me, of course? Like Talbot's?" he asked blandly.

"You'll find it in an envelope in my coat pocket, along with his passport, stateroom key, and tickets. You'd better fix it on now."

The situation was here. It just had to be accepted. He fished the envelope out quickly, patted the beard in place, then hesitated.

"Don't bother about me," Keiris assured him. "I can jet the ship back without trouble. I'm going to bury—them— in deep space. Then I'm going on in to Earth to check on something at the central morgue."

He was only half listening. "Keiris, if you were only the

wife of a man other than Kennicot Muir—or if I thought he were dead—"

"Don't miss the *Phobos*."

He gave her one last remembering look, then turned silently and vanished down the hatchway. She heard the space lock spin shut.

"Goodbye, darling," she whispered, knowing that she would never see him alive again.

E VER BEEN ON the sun before, Dr. Talbot?" Captain Andrews appraised the new passenger curiously. They were together in the observation room of the *Phobos.*

Alar could not admit that everything on the run from Luna to Mercury (which planet they had left an hour ago) had seemed tantalizingly familiar, as though he had made the trip not once but a hundred times. Nor could he admit that astrophysics was his profession. A certain amount of celestial ignorance would be forgiven—indeed required—in a historian.

"No," said the Thief. "This is my first trip."

"I thought perhaps I'd brought you out before. Your face seems vaguely familiar."

"Do you think so, Captain? I travel quite a bit on Earth. At a Toynbeean lecture possibly?"

"No. Never go to them. It would have to be somewhere along the solar run or nothing. Imagination, I guess."

Alar writhed inwardly. How far could he push his questioning without arousing suspicion? He stroked his false goatee with nervous impatience.

"As a newcomer," continued Captain Andrews, "you might be interested in how we pick up a solarion." He pointed to a circular fluorescent plate in the control panel.

"That gives us a running picture of the solar surface in terms of the H line of calcium Two—ionized calcium, that is.

"It shows where the solar prominences and faculae are because they carry a lot of calcium. You can't see any prominences on the plate here—they're only visible when they're on the limb of the sun, spouting up against black space. But here are plenty of faculae, these gassy little puffs floating above the photosphere—they can be detected almost to the center of the sun's disc. Hot but harmless."

He tapped the glass with his space-nav parallels. "And the place is swarming with granules—'solar thunderheads' might be a better name. They bubble up several hundred miles in five minutes and then vanish. If one of them ever caught the *Phobos* . . ."

"I had a cousin, Robert Talbot, who was lost on one of the early solar freighters," said Alar casually. "They always thought a solar storm must have got the ship."

"Very likely. We lost quite a few ships before we learned the proper approach. Your cousin, eh? Probably it was he I was thinking of, though I can't say the name is familiar."

"It was some years ago," said Alar, watching Andrews from the corner of his eye, "when Kennicot Muir was still running the stations."

"Hmm. Don't recall him." Captain Andrews returned noncommittally to the plate. "You probably know that the stations work at the edges of a sunspot, in what we call the penumbra. That procedure has several advantages.

"It's a little cooler than the rest of the chromosphere, which is easier on the solarion refrigerating system and the men, and the spot also provides a landmark for incoming freighters. It would be just about impossible to find a station unless it were on a spot. It's hard enough to locate one on the temperature contour."

"Temperature contour?"

"Yes—like a thirty-fathom line on a seacoast. Only here it's the five-thousand line. In a few minutes, when we're

about to land, I'll throw the jets over on automatic spectrographic steering and the *Phobos* will nose along the five-
thousand degree Kelvin contour until she finds Solarion
Nine."

"I see. If a station ever lost its lateral jets and couldn't
stay on the five-thousand line, how would you find it?"

"I wouldn't," said Captain Andrews curtly. "Whenever
a station turns up missing, we always send out all our search
boats—several hundred of them—and work a search pattern
around that sunspot for months. But we know before we
start that we won't find anything. We never have. It's futile
to look on the surface for a station that has been long volati-
lized deep at the vortex of a sunspot.

"The stations are under automatic spectrographic control, of course, and the spec is supposed to keep them on the
five-thousand line, but sometimes something goes wrong
with the spec or an unusually hot Wilson gas swirl spills out
over the edge of the spot and fools the spec into thinking the
station is standing way out from the spot, say on the hotter
five-thousand four hundred line.

"So the automatic spec control moves the station farther in toward the spot, maybe into the slippery Evershed
zone at its very lip. From there the station can slide on into
the umbra. I know of one ship that crawled out of the
Evershed. Its crew had to be replaced in toto. But no solarion ever came out of the umbra. So you can't rely entirely
on the spec control.

"Every station carries three solar meteorologists, too,
and the weather staff issues a bulletin every quarter-hour on
the station's most probable position and on any distur-
bances moving their way. Sometimes they have to jump fast
and in the right direction.

"And even the finest sunmen can't foresee everything.
Four years ago the Three, Four and Eight were working a
big 'leader'—spots are like poles in a magnet—always go in
pairs, and we call the eastern spot the 'leader,' the western
one the 'follower'—when the Mercury observatory noticed
the leader was rapidly growing smaller.

"By the time it occurred to the observatory what was happening, the spot had shrunk to the size of Connecticut County. The patrol ship they sent to take off the crews got there too late. The spot had vanished. They figured the stations would try to make it to the 'follower' and settle somewhere in its five-thousand line.

"The Eight did—barely. Luckily, it had been working the uppermost region of the leader and, when the spot vanished from beneath it, it had to drift down toward the solar equator. But while it was drifting it was also crawling back toward the follower with its lateral jets and it finally caught the follower's southern tip."

"What about the other two stations?" said Alar.

"No trace."

The Thief shrugged mental shoulders. A berth in a solarion wasn't exactly like retiring on the green benches of La Paz. He had never had any illusions about that. Perhaps the Mind had considered the possibilities of his survival in a solarion purely on cold statistics.

The captain moved away from the fluorescent plate toward a metal cabinet bolted to the far wall. He turned his head, spoke over his shoulder. "A glass of foam, doctor?"

Alar nodded. "Yes, thank you."

The captain unsnapped the door, fished in the shelves, withdrew a plastic bottle with one hand. With his other hand he found two aluminum cups.

"Sorry I can't offer you wine," the captain said, coming back across the cabin and setting the bottle and cups down on a small circular table. "This foam doesn't have any kick to it, but it's cold and that's plenty welcome in a place like this." His tone was faintly ironic. He poured out two drinks by squeezing the bottle, ejecting the liquid in a creamy ribbon that settled slowly in the cups. Then he took the bottle back to the refrigerated cabinet. The door slammed shut under a swipe from a huge hand.

Alar raised his cup and tasted the beverage. It had a sharp lemon taste, cold and spicy.

The Thief said, "It's delicious." He wasn't certain, but

he seemed to have remembered tasting it before. That could have been just a similarity to one of the more common refreshments he'd had during the past five years. Then again, it might have been for another reason . . .

The captain smacked his lips. "I've unlimited quantities of it, I drink it often and I never tire of it." He looked into the cup. "I've got boxes of it in my quarters. Little dehydrated pills. When a bottle's empty, I just drop in a pill, squirt in some drinking water and let it get cold. Then," he snapped his fingers, "I've got a new supply." He was as much in earnest speaking of his foam as he had been in describing the operation of the solarions.

"I assume you've briefed yourself on the history of our stations," Captain Andrews said abruptly. He indicated a tubular chair for Alar, kicked another one over to the table for himself.

"Yes, I have, Captain."

"Good."

Alar recognized an undertone behind the succinctness of the question and the comment. Sunmen didn't relive the past. The past was too morbid. Of the twenty-seven costly solarions, towed one by one to the sun during the past ten years, sixteen remained. The average life of a station was about a year. The staff was rotated continuously, each man, after long and arduous training, being assigned a post for sixty days—three times the twenty-day synodic period of rotation of the sun with respect to the eighty-eight-day sidereal period of Mercury.

The captain finished his drink and took Alar's empty cup. "I'll clean them later," he said as he put one inside the other and replaced them in the cabinet. He resumed his seat again, heavily, and asked, "Have you met the replacements?"

"Not yet," Alar said. When the Mercury observatory reached opposition with a given solar station, as it did every twenty days, a freighter carried in replacements for one-third of the staff and took away the oldest one-third along with a priceless cargo of muirium. The *Phobos*, he knew, was bringing in eleven replacements, but so far they had confined themselves closely to their own quarter of the ship, and he had been unable to meet any of them.

Captain Andrews had apparently dismissed the problem of Alar's pseudo-familiarity, and the Thief could think of no immediate way to return to the subject. For the time being he would have to continue to be Dr. Talbot, the historian, ignorant of things solar.

"Why," he asked, "if the stations are in such continual danger, aren't they equipped with full space drives, instead of weak lateral jets? Then, if the station skidded into a spot beyond the present recovery point, she could simply blast free."

Andrews shook his head. "Members of parliament have been elected and deposed on that very issue. But it has to be the way it is now when you consider the cost of the solarion. It's really just a vast synthesizer for making muirium with a little bubble of space in the middle for living quarters and a few weak lateral jets on the periphery.

"A space ship is all converter, with a little bubble here amidships for the crew. To make a space ship out of a solarion you'd have to build it about two hundred times the present solarion size, so that the already tremendous solarion would be just a little bubble in an unimaginably enormous space ship.

"There's always a lot of talk about making the stations safe, but that's the only way to do it and it costs too much money. So the Spaceways Ministers rise and fall, but the stations never change. Incidentally, on the cost of these things, I understand that about one-fourth of the annual Imperium budget goes into making one solarion."

The intercom buzzed. Andrews excused himself, answered it briefly, then replaced the instrument. "Doctor?" The officer seemed strangely troubled.

"Yes, captain?" His heart held no warning beat, but it was impossible not to realize that something unusual and serious was in store.

Andrews hesitated a moment as though he were about

to speak. Then he lifted his shoulders helplessly. "As you know, I'm carrying a relief crew to Nine—your destination. You haven't met any of them before because they keep pretty much to themselves. They would like to see you in the mess—now."

It was clear to Alar that the man wanted to say more, perhaps give him a word of warning.

"Why do they want to see me?" he asked bluntly.

Andrews was equally curt. "They'll explain." He cleared his throat and avoided Alar's arched eyebrows. "You aren't superstitious, are you?"

"I think not. Why do you ask?"

"I just wondered. It's best not to be superstitious. We'll land in a few minutes, and I'm going to be pretty busy. The catwalk on the left will take you to the mess."

The Thief frowned, stroked his false goatee, then turned and walked toward the exit panel.

"Oh, doctor," called Andrews.

"Yes, captain?"

"Just in case I don't see you again I've discovered whom you remind me of."

"Who?"

"This man was taller, heavier and older than you, and his hair was auburn while yours is black. And he's dead, anyway, so really there's no point in mentioning—"

"Kennicot Muir?"

"Yes." Andrews looked after him rather meditatively.

Always Muir! If the man were alive and could be found, what an inquisition he would face! Alar's footsteps clanged in hollow frustration as he strode across the catwalk over an empty decontaminated muirium hold.

Muir must certainly have been on the *T-22* when it crashed at the end of its weird journey backward in time; the log book was evidence of that. But he, Alar, had crawled out of the river carrying the book. What had happened to Muir? Had he gone down with the ship? Alar chewed his lower lip in exasperation.

There was a more immediate question—what did the relief crew want with him? He welcomed the chance to meet them, but he wanted to be the one to ask questions. He felt off-balance.

What if one of the crew had known the true Dr. Talbot? And, of course, any of the eleven might be an I.P. in occupational disguise, warned to be on the lookout for him. Or perhaps they didn't want him along on general principles. After all, he was an uninvited outsider who might disturb the smooth teamwork so necessary to their hourly survival.

Or possibly they had invited him in for a little hazing, which he understood was actually encouraged by the station psychiatrist for the relief of tension in new men, so long as it was done and over before they came on station.

As he left the catwalk for the narrow corridor, he heard music and laughter ahead.

He smiled. A party. He remembered now that the incoming shift always gave themselves a farewell party, the main features of which were mournful, interminable and nonprintable ballads, mostly concerning why they had left Terra to take up their present existence—new and unexpurgated holographic movies of dancing girls clothed mainly with varihued light (personal gift of the Minister for Space), pretzels and beer.

Only beer, because they had to check into the station cold sober. Two months later, if their luck held, they'd throw another party on the *Phobos,* and the *Phobos* crew would join in. Even the staid, blunt Andrews would upend a couple of big ones in toasting their safe return.

But not now. The outgoing festivities were strictly private—for sunmen only. No strangers were ever invited. Even an incoming station psychiatrist was excluded.

What then? Something was wrong.

As he stood poised to knock on the door, he found himself counting his pulse. It throbbed at one hundred fifty and was climbing.

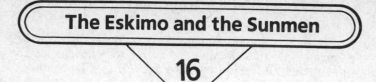

The Eskimo and the Sunmen

16

ALAR STOOD AT the door, counting out the rapid rise of his pulse, considering what he might have to face on the other side. His knuckled hand dropped in an instinctive motion toward a non-existent saber pommel. Weapons were forbidden on the *Phobos*. But what danger could there be in such self-commiserating good fellowship? Still, suppose they tried a little horseplay and yanked at his false beard? While he hesitated, the music and laughter died away.

Then the ship lurched awkwardly, and he was thrown against the door. The *Phobos* had nosed into Solarion Nine and was sealing herself to the entry ports. A wild cheer from within the mess rose above his crash against the door.

Whether they hailed the survival of the station or their own imminent departure he could not be sure. There was something mocking and sardonic about the ovation that led him to suspect the latter. Let the old shift do their own cheering.

"Come in!" boomed someone.

He pushed the door aside and walked in.

Ten faces looked at him expectantly. Two of the younger men were sitting by the holograph, but the translucent cube that contained the tri-di image was dark. It had evidently just been turned off.

144

Two men were returning from a table laden with a beer keg, several large wooden pretzel bowls, beer mugs, napkins, ash trays and other bric-a-brac, and were headed toward the dining table nearest the Thief. At the table, six men were in the act of rising. The missing eleventh face was probably the psychiatrist—absent by mutual understanding and consent.

The party was over, he sensed uneasily. This was something different.

"Dr. Talbot," said the large florid man with the booming voice, "I'm Miles, incoming station master for the Nine."

Alar nodded silently.

"And this is my meteorologist, Williams—MacDougall, lateral jet pilot—Florez, spectroscopist—Saint Claire, production engineer. . . ."

The Thief acknowledged the introductions gravely but noncommittally, down to young Martinez, clerk. His eyes missed nothing. These men were all repeaters. At some time in the past they had all oozed cold sweat in a solar station, probably most of them at different times and in different stations. But the common experience had branded them, welded them together and cast them beyond the pale of their earthbound brothers.

The twenty eyes had never left his face. What did they expect of him?

He folded his hands inconspicuously and counted his pulse. It had leveled off at one-sixty.

Miles resumed his rumble: "Dr. Talbot, we understand that you are going to be with us for twenty days."

Alar almost smiled. Miles, as a highly skilled and unconsciously snobbish sunman of long experience, held in profound contempt any unit of time less than a full and dangerous sixty days' shift.

"I have requested the privilege," returned the Thief gravely. "I hope you haven't decided that I'll be in the way."

"Not at all."

"The Toynbeean Institute has long been anxious to have a professional historian prepare a monograph—"

"Oh, we don't care *why* you're coming, Dr. Talbot. And don't worry about getting in our way. You look as though you have sense enough to stay clear when we're busy and you'll be worth your weight in unitas if you can keep the psych happily occupied and out of our laps. You play chess, I hope? This psych we have is an eskimo."

He couldn't remember having heard the term "Eskimo" applied to a sunman before, and he was astonished that he understood its meaning, which seemed to spring to mind unbidden, as though from the mental chamber that contained his other life. He had made no mistake in deciding to board the *Phobos*. But for the moment he must pretend ignorance.

"Chess—Eskimo?" he murmured with puzzled politeness.

Several of the men smiled.

"Sure, Eskimo," boomed Miles impatiently. "Never been in a solarion before. Has the sweat he was born with. Probably fresh out of school and loaded down with chess sets to keep our minds occupied so we won't brood." He laughed suddenly, harshly. "So we won't brood! Great flaming faculae! Why do they think we keep coming back here?"

Alar realized that the hair was crawling on his neck and that his armpits were wet. And he knew now what common brand had marked these lost souls and joined them into an outré brotherhood.

As the real Talbot had surmised that night at the ball, *every one of these creatures was stark mad!*

"I'll try to keep the psych occupied," he agreed with plausible dubiousness. "I rather like a game of chess myself."

"Chess!" murmured Florez, the spectroscopist, with dispassionate finality, turning from Alar to stare wearily at the table. His complete absence of venom did not mute his meaning.

Miles laughed again and fixed Alar with bloodshot eyes. "But we didn't invite you here simply to ask you to get the psych out of our hair. The fact is, all ten of us are Indians— old sunmen. And that's unusual. Generally we have at least one Eskimo in the bunch."

The big man's hand flashed into his pocket and two dice clattered along the table toward the Thief. There was a sharp intake of breath somewhere down the table. Alar thought it was Martinez, the young clerk. Everyone pressed slowly on either side of the table toward their guest and the white cubes that lay before him.

"Will you please pick them up, Dr. Talbot?" demanded Miles.

Alar hesitated. What would the action commit him to?

"Go on," Martinez said, impatient and eager. "Go on, sir."

The Thief studied the dice. A little worn, perhaps, but completely ordinary. He reached out slowly, gathered them into his right hand. He raised his hand and opened his fingers so that they rested side by side on his palm almost under Miles's nose.

"Well?"

"Ah," Miles said. "And now I suppose I should inform you of the significance of what you'll soon do for us."

"I'm very interested," Alar replied. He wondered at the form the ritual was about to take. That it was a ritual of immense import to the men he did not doubt.

"When we have a genuine Eskimo, Dr. Talbot, we ask him to throw the dice."

"You have your choice, then? I believe the psychiatrist would qualify, wouldn't he?"

"Huh," grunted the incoming station master. "Sure, the psych's an Eskimo, but all psychs are poison."

"I see." Alar closed his fist over the cubes.

"Martinez could do the honors, too, for that matter. Martinez has served only two shifts and he hasn't really crowded his luck too far to disqualify him. But we don't want to use him if we can help it."

"So logically I'm it."

"Right. The rest of us are no good. Florez is next lowest with five shifts. This would be his sixth—utterly impossible, of course. And so on up to me, with full ten years' service. I'm the Jonah. I can't roll 'em. That leaves you. You're not really an Eskimo—you'll be with us only twenty days—but several of us old timers have decided it'll be legal because you resemble an old friend."

Muir, of course. It was fantastic. The Thief aroused himself as though from a heavy dream. The dice felt cold and weightless in his numbing fist. And his heart beat was climbing again.

He cleared his throat. "May I ask what happens after I roll the dice?"

"Nothing—immediately," replied Miles. "We just file out, grab our gear, and walk up the ramp into the station."

It couldn't be that simple. Martinez's mouth was hanging open as though his life depended on this. Florez was hardly breathing. And so on around the table. Even Miles seemed more flushed than when Alar had entered the room.

He thought furiously. Was it a gamble involving some tremendous sum that he was deciding? The sunmen were bountifully paid. Perhaps they had pooled their earnings and he was to decide the winner.

"Will you hurry yourself, *por favor*, Dr. Talbot?" said Martinez faintly.

This was something bigger than money. Alar rattled the dice loosely in his hand and let them go.

And in the act a belated warning seemed to bubble up from his fogged preamnesic life. He clawed futilely at the cubes but it was too late. A three and a four.

He had just condemned a solarion crew—and himself—to death.

Alar exchanged glances with Martinez, who had suddenly become very pale.

A solarion dies once a twelvemonth, so a sunman on a

two-month shift has one chance in six of dying with it. Florez couldn't make the throw because this would be his sixth shift, and by the laws of chance, his time was up.

One in six—these madmen were positive that a roll of the dice could predict a weary return to Terra—or a vaporous grave on the sun.

One chance in six. There had been one chance in six of throwing a seven. His throw would kill these incredible fanatics just as surely as if he cut them down with a Kades. These ten would walk into the solarion knowing that they would die, and sooner or later one of them would subconsciously commit the fatal error that would send the station plunging down into the sunspot vortex, or adrift on the uncharted, unfathomable photosphere. And he would be along.

It seemed that everyone, for a queer unearthly hiatus, had stopped breathing. Martinez was moving pallid lips, but no sound was coming out.

Indeed, no one said anything at all. There was nothing to say.

Miles thoughtfully thrust an enormous black cigar into his mouth, pushed his chair back to the table, and walked slowly from the room without a backward glance. The others followed, one by one.

Alar waited a full five minutes after the footsteps had died away toward the ramp that led up into Solarion Nine, full of wonder both at his stupidity and at the two tantalizing flashes from his other life.

His death was certain if he followed them into the solarion. But he couldn't hang back now. He recalled the Mind's prediction. It had been a calculated risk.

His main regret was that he was now *persona non grata* to the crew. It would be a long time before he learned anything from these fanatics—probably not before one of them destroyed the station. But it couldn't have been helped.

He stepped into the corridor, looked toward the ramp a dozen yards away and sucked in his breath sharply. Four

I.P.'s favored him with stony stares, then, as one man, drew their sabers.

Then a horrid, unforgettable giggle bit at his unbelieving left ear.

"Small solar system, eh, Thief?"

Visitors are not allowed in this portion of the morgue, madame. There's nothing here but unclaimed bodies." The gray-clad slave attendant barring her way bowed unctuously but firmly.

The only sign of Keiris's impatience was a faint dilation of the nostrils. "There are one thousand unitas in this envelope," she said quietly, indicating the packet fastened beneath her cape clasp. "I will need only thirty seconds within the cubicle. Unlock the door."

The slave eyed the envelope hungrily and swallowed nervously. His eyes studied the hall behind the woman.

"A thousand unitas isn't much. If I got caught, it would mean my life."

"It's all I have." She noted with alarm the man's growing firmness.

"Then you can't go in." He folded his arms before his chest.

"Do you want your freedom?" demanded Keiris abruptly. "I can tell you how to get it. You need only take me alive. I am Madame Haze-Gaunt."

The slave gaped at her.

She continued swiftly. "The chancellor has offered a billion-unita reward for my capture. Enough," she added caustically, "to buy your freedom and set yourself up as a great slave-holder. All you have to do is lock me in the cubicle behind you and notify the police."

Was it worth this to her? A few moments would tell.

"But don't cry out before you let me into the room," she warned quietly. "If you do, I have a knife with which I will kill myself. Then you will not get the billion unitas. Instead, they will kill you."

The attendant gasped something incomprehensible. At last his trembling fingers got the keys from his pocket. After several false tries, he finally succeeded in unlocking the door.

Keiris stepped inside quickly. The door locked behind her. She looked about her quickly. The tiny room, like the thousands of others on this level, contained but one thing—a cheap transparent plastic casket resting on a waist-high wooden platform.

A strange feeling came over Keiris. It seemed to her that her whole life revolved around what she would learn in the next few seconds. Even the Mind, for all his detailing scrutiny, had probably never thought of checking the morgue. After all, the *T-22* Log mentioned only two living things, both of which had been identified as Alar and Haze-Gaunt's ape-creature.

For the moment she avoided looking at what was inside, but instead read the printed and framed legend resting on the upper surface:

Unidentified and unclaimed. Recovered by Imperial River Police from the Ohio River near Wheeling on July 21, 2172.

Would it be Kim?
Finally Keiris forced herself to look into the casket.
It was not Kim.
It was a woman. The body was loosely clad from toes to breasts in thin mortuary gauze. The face was pale and thin and the translucent skin was drawn tightly over the rather

high cheekbones. The long hair was black except for a broad white streak streaming from the forehead.

A key was turning in the lock behind her. Let them come.

The door burst open. Someone, in the ungrammatical terseness of the well-trained I.P., said, "It's her."

She had time for only one more look at the corpse, one more look at its armless shoulders, one more look at the knife buried in its heart—a knife identical to the one she now carried in the sheath on her left thigh.

The meaning of the four guards at the ramp was now only too clear to the Thief. Shey had put them there. Others were undoubtedly behind him.

Shey, then, must be Miles's "Eskimo psych"—and with animal cunning the little man had been waiting for Alar on the *Phobos* ever since its arrival on the moon.

But instead of feeling trapped the Thief felt only elated. At least, before he died, he would have an opportunity to punish Shey.

Shey's present precautions would certainly have been enough to recapture an ordinary fugitive, but the same was true of the other traps that had been laid for Alar. The wolf pack was still proceeding on the assumption that methods applicable to human beings, enlarged and elaborated perhaps, were equally applicable to him. He believed now that their premise was wrong.

The image of Keiris's preternatural slenderness flashed before him. Yes, the time had come to punish Shey. His oath as a Thief prevented his killing the psychologist, but justice permitted other remedies, which could best be administered aboard the solarion. His pursuer had doubtless expected to capture him here and almost certainly had no intention of risking that august hide in a solarion. That was about to be changed.

He turned slowly, bracing himself mentally for the photic blast to come.

"Do you see this finger, Shey?" He held his right forefinger erect midway on the line joining his eyes with the psychologist's.

By pure reflex action Shey's pupils focused on the finger. Then his neck jerked imperceptibly as a narrow 'x' of blue-white light exploded from Alar's eyes into his.

The next five seconds would tell whether the Thief's gambling attempt at hypnosis by overstimulation of the other's optical sensorium had been successful.

"I am Dr. Talbot of the Toynbeean Institute," he whispered rapidly. "You are the incoming psych for the solarion Nine. We'll board together. As we approach the guards on the ramp tell them everything is all right and ask them to bring in our gear immediately." Shey blinked at him.

Would it really work? Was it too preposterous? Had he been insanely overconfident?

The Thief wheeled and walked briskly toward the ramp and the watchful I.P.'s. Behind him came the sound of running feet.

"Stop!" cried Shey, hurrying up with his other four guards.

Alar bit his lip indecisively. He had evidently lost the gamble. If Shey planned to have him killed on the spot, he should try to break past the swordsmen on the ramp into the solarion. A means of escape might open up in the resulting confusion. Undoubtedly Miles would not submit tamely to Shey's forcible invasion.

"Don't harm that man!" called Shey. "He's not the one."

He had done it.

"Well, Dr. Talbot," giggled Shey, "what is the Toynbeean opinion of life in a solarion on this July twentieth?"

Alar pushed himself away from the table in Shey's private dining room and stroked his false goatee thoughtfully. His smile held a faint curl. "My first thought, sir, is that it is most generous of you to volunteer for such risky duty."

Shey frowned, then giggled. "A last-minute whim,

really. Originally I was merely trying to contact a chap on Lunar Station . . ." He uttered a puzzled, gurgling bray evidently intended as a laugh. "But then I had this sudden conviction that I should try to help these poor devils on Solarion Nine. And here I am."

Alar shook his head. "Actually, Count, I'm afraid they're beyond aid. I've been here only forty-eight hours, but I've come to the conclusion that a sixty-day shift in a solarion ruins a man for life. He comes in fresh and sane. He leaves insane."

"I agree, doctor, but doesn't this deterioration in the individual have a larger significance to a Toynbeean?"

"Very possibly," admitted the Thief judicially. "But first, let us examine a society of some thirty souls, cast away from the mother culture and cooped up in a solarion. Vast dangers threaten on every side. If the Fraunhofer man should fail to catch an approaching calcium facula in time to warn the lateral jet man—bang—the station goes.

"If the apparatus that prevents solar radiation from volatilizing the station by continuously converting the radiation into muirium should jam for a split second—whoosh—no more station. Or say the freighter fails to show up and cart the muirium away from the stock rooms, forcing us to turn muirium back into the sun—another bang.

"Or suppose our weatherman fails to notice a slight increase in magnetic activity and our sunspot suddenly decides to enlarge itself in our direction with free sliding to the sun's core. Or suppose the muirium anti-grav drive breaks down upstairs, and we have nothing to hold us up against the sun's twenty-seven G's. Or let the refrigeration system fail for ten minutes . . .

"You can see, Count Shey, that it is the normal lot of people who must live this life to be—by terrestrial standards—insane. Insanity under such conditions is a useful and logical defense mechanism, an invaluable and salutary retreat from reality.

"Until the crew makes this adjustment—'response to

challenge of environment' as we Toynbeeans call it—they have little chance of survival. The will to insanity in a sun-man is as vital as the will to irrigate in a Sumerian. But perhaps I encroach on the psychologist's field."

Shey smirked. "Though I can't agree with you entirely, doctor, still you may have something. Would you say, then, that the *raison d'être* of a solarion psychiatrist is to drive the men toward madness?"

"I can answer that question by asking another," replied Alar, eyeing his quarry covertly. "Let us suppose a norm for existence has been established in a given society. If one or two of the group deviate markedly from the norm, we say they are insane.

"And yet the whole society may be considered insane by a foreign culture which may consider the one or two recalcitrants the only sane persons in the model society. So can't we define sanity as conformity to—and belief in—the norm of whatever culture we represent?"

Shey pursed his lips. "Perhaps."

"And then, if a few of the crew can't lose themselves in a retreat from the peril of their daily existence—if they can't cling to some saving certainty, even if it is only the certainty of near death—or if they can't find some other illusion that might make existence bearable—isn't it your duty to make these or other forms of madness easy for them? To teach them the rudiments of insanity, as it were?"

Shey sniggered uneasily. "In a moment you'll have me believing that in an asylum, the only lunatic is the psychologist."

Alar regarded him placidly as he held up his wine glass. "Do you realize, my dear Count, that you have repeated your last sentence not once but twice? Do you think I am hard of hearing?" He sipped at his wine casually.

Startled disbelief showed in the psychologist's face. "You imagined that I repeated myself. I distinctly remember—"

"Of course, of course. No doubt I misunderstood you." Alar lifted his shoulders in a delicate apology. "But," he pressed, "suppose you *had* repeated yourself and then denied it. In a layman you'd probably analyze such fixation on trivia as incipient paranoia, to be followed in due time by delusions of persecution.

"In you, of course, it's hardly worth consideration. If it happened at all it was probably just an oversight. A couple of days on one of these stations is enough to disorganize almost anyone." He put his wine glass down on the table gently. "Nothing in your room has been trifled with lately?" He had slipped into Shey's quarters the previous day and had rotated every visible article 180 degrees.

Shey giggled nervously. Finally he said, "Certainly not."

"Then there's nothing to worry about." Alar patted his goatee amiably. "While we're on the subject, you might tell me something. As a Toynbeean, I have always been interested in how one person determines whether another is sane or insane. I understand you psychologists actually have cut-and-dried tests of sanity."

Shey looked across the table at him narrowly, then chuckled. "Ah, sanity—no, there's no simple book test for that, but I do have some projection slides that evaluate one's motor and mental integration. Such evaluation, of course, is not without bearing on the question of sanity, at least sanity as *I* understand it. Would you care to run through a few of them with me?"

Alar nodded politely. Shey, he knew, wanted to run the slides more to reassure himself than to entertain his guest.

The psychologist was due for the rudest shock of his life.

Shey quickly set up the holograph and projector screen. "We'll start with some interesting maze slides," he chirped, switching off the light that dangled from the ceiling hook. "The ability to solve mazes quickly is strongly correlated to analyses of our daily problems. The faltering maze-solver unravels his difficulties piecemeal and lacks the cerebral integration that characterizes the executive.

"It is interesting to note that the schizophrenic can

solve only the simplest mazes, even after repeated trials. So here's the first and simplest. White rats solve it—laid out on the floor with walls, of course—after three or four runs. A child of five, viewing it as we shall here, gets it in about thirty seconds. Adults instantaneously."

"Quite obvious," agreed Alar coolly as he projected a false opening in the outer maze border and covered the real one with a section of false border.

Shey stirred uneasily, but apparently considered his inability to solve the maze as a passing mental quirk. He switched slides.

"What's the average time on this next one?" asked Alar. "Ten seconds."

The Thief let the second and third ones go by without photic alteration. Shey's relief was plain even in the darkness.

But on the fourth slide Alar alternately opened and blocked various passages of the maze, and he knew that Shey, standing beside the projector, was rubbing his eyes. The little psychologist sighed gratefully when his guest suggested leaving the maze series and trying something else.

The Thief smiled.

"Our second series of slides, Dr. Talbot, shows a circle and an ellipse side by side. On each successive slide—there are twelve—the ellipse becomes more and more circular. Persons of the finest visual discrimination can detect the differences on all twelve cards. Dogs can detect two, apes four, six-year-old children ten, and the average man eleven. Keep your own score. Here's the first one."

A large white circle showed on a black screen, and near the circle was a narrow ellipse. That was pretty obvious. Alar decided to wait for the next one.

On the second slide Shey frowned, removed it from the projector, held it up to the light of the screen, then inserted it once again. On the third slide he began to chew his lips. But he kept on. When the tenth was reached he was perspiring profusely and licking sweat from the edges of his mouth.

The Thief continued to make noncommittal acknowledgments as each slide was presented. He felt no pity whatever for Shey, who had no means of knowing that from the second slide on, there were no ellipses, only pairs of identical circles. Each ellipse had been cancelled by a projection from Alar's eyes, and a circle substituted.

Shey made no motion to insert the eleventh slide in the projector. He said, "Shall we stop here? I think you've got the general idea . . ."

Alar nodded. "Very interesting. What else have you?"

His host hesitated, apparently fumbling with the projector housing. Finally he giggled glassily. "I have some Rorschachs. They're more or less conventionalized but they serve to reveal psychosis in its formative stages."

"If this is tiring you—" began Alar with diabolical tact.

"Not at all."

The Thief smiled grimly.

The screen lit up again, and the rotund psychologist held a slide up to its light for a lengthy inspection. Then he slid the slide into the projector. He commented, "To a normal person, the first slide resembles a symmetrical silhouette of two ballet dancers, or two skipping children, or sometimes two dogs playing. Psychotics, of course, see something they consider fearful or macabre, such as a tarantula, a demoniacal mask or a—"

Alar had smoothly transformed the image into a grinning skull. "Rather like a couple of dancers, isn't it?" he observed.

Shey pulled out his handkerchief and ran it over his face. The second slide he inserted without comment, but Alar could hear it rattle as trembling fingers dropped it into the projector.

"Looks rather like two trees," observed the Thief meditatively, "or perhaps two feathers, or possibly two rivulets flowing together in a meadow. What would a psychotic see?"

Shey was standing mute and motionless, apparently more dead than alive. He seemed to be aware of nothing in the room but the image within the screen, and Alar sensed that the man was staring at it in fascinated horror. He would have given a great deal to steal a look at the creature whose warped mind he was destroying, but he thought it best to continue transforming the image.

"What would a madman see?" he repeated quietly.

Shey's whisper was unrecognizable. "A pair of white arms."

Alar reached over, flicked off the projector and screen and stole quietly from the darkened room. His host never moved.

The Thief had not taken two steps down the corridor when a muffled gust of giggles welled out from the closed door—then another and another—finally so many that they merged into one another in a long pealing paroxysm.

He could still hear it when he turned the corridor corner toward his own stateroom. He stroked his goatee and smiled.

Station master Miles and Florez, who were arguing heatedly over something, passed him without acknowledging his polite bow or even his existence. He watched them thoughtfully until they turned the corner and vanished. Theirs was the ideal state of mind—to be mad and not know it. Their staunch faith in their inevitable destruction clothed them in an aura of purposeful sanity.

Without that faith, their mental disintegration would probably be swift and complete. Undoubtedly they would prefer to die rather than to leave the station alive at the end of their shift.

He wondered whether Shey would make an equally dramatic adjustment to his new-won madness.

Duel Ended

18

THE RACING OF his heart awoke him a few hours later in his room.

He listened tensely as he rose from his bunk. But there was no sound, other than the all-pervasive rumble of the vast and frenzied gases outside.

He dressed quickly, stepped to the door opening into the corridor, and looked down the hall. It was empty.

Queer—usually two or three men could be seen hurrying on some vital task or other. His heartbeat was up to one-eighty.

All he had to do was follow his unerring scent for danger. He stepped brusquely into the corridor and strode toward Shey's room. He arrived there in a moment and stood before the door, listening. No sound. He knocked curtly without result. He knocked again. Why didn't Shey answer? Was there a stealthy movement within the room?

His heartbeat touched one-eighty-five and was still climbing. His right hand flexed uneasily. Should he return for his saber?

He shook off an impulse to run back to his room. If there was danger here, at least it would be informative danger. Somehow, he doubted that a blade would influence the issue. He looked around him. The hall was still empty.

The preposterous thought occurred to him that he was

the only being left aboard. Then he smiled humorlessly. His fertile imagination was becoming too much even for himself. He seized the panel knob, turned it swiftly, and leaped into the room.

In the dim light, while his heartbeat soared toward two hundred, he beheld a number of things.

The first was Shey's bloated, insensate face, framed in curls, staring down at him about a foot beneath the central ceiling lamp hook. The abnormal protrusion of the eyes was doubtless caused by the narrow leather thong that stretched taut from the folds of the neck to the hook. To one side of the little man's dangling feet was the overturned projector table.

Beyond the gently swaying corpse, in front of the screen, Thurmond sat quietly, studying Alar with enigmatic eyes. On either side of the police minister a Kades gun was aimed at Alar's breast.

Each man seemed locked in the vise of the other's stare. Like capacitor plates, thought Alar queerly, with a corpse for a dielectric. For a long time the Thief had the strange illusion that he was part of a holo projection, that Thurmond would gaze at him with unblinking eyes forever, that he was safe because a Kades could not really be fired in holo projections.

The room swayed faintly under their feet as an exceptionally violent and noisy swirl of gas beat at the solarion. It aroused them both from their paralytic reveries.

Thurmond was the first to speak.

"In the past," came his dry, chill voice, "our traps for you were subject to the human equation. This factor no longer operates in your favor. If you move from where you now stand, the Kades will fire automatically."

Alar laughed shortly. "In times past, when you were positive you'd taken adequate precautions in your attempts to seize me, you were always proved wrong. I can see that your comrade's suicide has shaken you—otherwise you would have made no attempt to explain my prospective fate.

Your verbal review of your trap is mainly for your own assurance. Your expectation that I will die is a hope rather than a certainty. May I suggest that the circumstances hold as much danger for you as for me?"

His voice held a confidence he was far from feeling. He was undoubtedly boxed in by tell-tale devices, perhaps body capacitors or photocell relays, that activated the Kades. If he leaped at the man, he would simply float to the floor—a mass of sodden cinders.

Thurmond's brows contracted imperceptibly. "You were bluffing, of course, when you suggested the situation contained as much danger for me as for you, since you must die in any event, while my only sources of personal concern are the general considerations of danger aboard a solarion and interference from the crew.

"I have minimized the latter possibility by transferring to Mercury all but a skeleton crew—Miles's shift. And they're alerted to signal the *Phobos* and leave with me as soon as I return to the assembly room, which will be in about ten minutes." He arose almost casually, edged around the nearest Kades and sidled slowly along the wall toward the corridor panel, carefully avoiding the portion of the room covered by the guns.

Thurmond had demonstrated once again why Haze-Gaunt had invited him into the wolf pack. He relied on the leverage of titanic forces when he had difficulty in disposing of an obstacle, and damned the cost.

It was utterly simple. There would be no struggle, no personal combat. No immediate issue would be reached. And yet, within a satisfactorily short time, Alar would be dead. He couldn't move without triggering the two Kades, and there would be no one left to free him. The solarion would be evacuated within a few minutes. The crewless station would slide over the brim of the sunspot long before he would collapse from fatigue.

The wolf pack was willing to exchange one of its six most valuable munition factories for his life.

And yet—it wasn't enough. The Thief was now hardly breathing, because he believed he knew now what Miles and Florez had been discussing in the hall.

Thurmond was now at the panel, turning the knob slowly.

"Your program," said Alar softly, "is sound save in one rather obscure but important particular. Your indifference to Toynbeean principles would naturally blind you to the existence of such a factor as 'self-determination in a society.'"

The police minister paused the barest fraction of a second before stepping through the panel.

The Thief continued, "Can you make sense out of a Fraunhofer report? Can you operate a lateral jet motor? If not you'd better deactivate the Kades because you're going to need me badly, and very soon. You'll have no time to signal the *Phobos.*"

The police minister hesitated just outside the door.

"If," said Alar, "you think the skeleton crew under Miles is in present control of the station, you'd better take a look around."

There was no answer. Thurmond evidently thought that one would be superfluous. His footsteps died away down the hall.

Alar looked up quizzically at Shey's gorged and pop-eyed face, then at the two Kades. "He'll be back," he murmured, folding his arms.

And yet, when he heard the footsteps returning considerably faster than they had departed, this confirmation of his surmise concerning Andrews's crew threw him into a deep gloom. However, it had been inevitable. Nothing could have saved them after he threw the seven.

Thurmond walked quickly into the room. "You were right," he said. "Where have they hidden themselves?"

"They're in hiding," replied Alar without expression, "But not in the way you think. All ten of them were certain they were going to die on this shift. They had a fatalistic faith in their destiny. To return safely with you would have meant giving up that faith, with consequent mental and moral disintegration. They preferred to die. You'll probably find their bodies in the muirium holds."

Thurmond's mouth tightened. "You're lying."

"Having no historical background, you would naturally assume so. But regardless of what happened to Miles and his crew, you'll have to come to some decision about me within the next minute or two. We've been adrift in the Evershed zone ever since I entered the room. You can release me in order to let me have a try at the lateral jets, or you can leave me here—and die with me."

He watched the inward struggle in the police minister. Would the man's personal loyalty to Haze-Gaunt, or perhaps a chill adamantine sense of duty, require him to keep Alar immobilized at the cost of his own life?

Thurmond toyed thoughtfully with the pommel of his breast dagger. "All right," he said finally. Passing behind the Kades, he snapped the switches on each. "You'd better hurry. It's safe now."

"Shey's scabbard and blade are on the table beside you," said the Thief. "Give them to me."

Thurmond permitted himself a smile as he handed over the saber. Alar knew the man planned to kill him as soon as the station was safe again and that it mattered little to the greatest swordsman in the Imperium whether the Thief was armed.

"A question," the Thief said as he buckled the scabbard to his belt. "Were you on the *Phobos* along with Shey?"

"I was on the *Phobos*. But not with Shey. I let him try his own plan first."

"And when he failed—"

"I acted."

"One other question," insisted the Thief imperturbably. "How did you and Shey know where to find me?"

"The Meganet Mind."

It was incomprehensible. The Mind alternately condemned him and delivered him. Why? Why? Would he never know?

"All right," he said shortly. "Come along."

Together they hurried toward the control room.

An hour later they emerged, perspiring freely.

Alar turned and studied his arch-enemy briefly. He said: "Obviously, I can't permit you to signal the *Phobos* until my own status has been clarified to my satisfaction. I see no particular advantage in delaying what has been inevitable since our first meeting." He drew his saber with cold deliberation, hoping that his measured certainty would create an impression on Thurmond.

The police minister whipped out his own blade. "You are quite right. You had to die in either event. To save my life I justifiably relied on your desire to prolong your own. *Die!*"

As in many occasions in the past when death faced him, time began to creep by the Thief, and he observed Thurmond's cry of doom and simultaneous lunge as part of a leisurely acted play. Thurmond's move was an actor's part to be studied, analyzed and constructively criticized by responsive words and gestures of his own, well organized and harmoniously knit.

He knew, without reflecting on the quality of mind that permitted and required him to know, that Thurmond's shout and lunge were not meant to kill him. Thurmond's *fleche* was apparently, "high line right," which, if successful, would thrust through Alar's heart and right lung. Experts conventionally parried such a thrust with an ordinary *tierce*, or perhaps a *quinte*, and followed with a riposte toward the opponent's groin.

Yet there had been a speculative, questioning element in Thurmond's cry. The man had evidently expected the Thief to perceive his deceit, to realize that he had planned a highly intricate composite attack based on Alar's almost reflexive response to the high line thrust, and the skilled Thief would be expected to upset a possible trap by the simple expedient of locking blades and starting anew.

This analysis of the attack was plausible except for one thing: Thurmond, never one to take unavoidable risks, instead of unlocking blades, would very likely seize his breast dagger and drive it into his opponent's throat.

Yet the Thief could not simultaneously cut the dagger scabbard away and avoid the lunge.

Then suddenly everything was past. Thurmond had sprung back, spitting malevolently, and the dagger scabbard was spinning crazily through the air behind him. A streak of red was growing rapidly along the Thief's chest. The police minister laughed lightly.

Alar's heart was beating very fast—just how fast he did not know—pumping its vital substance through the deceptively simple cut in his lung. It couldn't have been helped. Now, if he could maim or disarm Thurmond fairly quickly, he might still summon the *Phobos* and escape under the protection of Captain Andrews before he died of loss of blood.

His skilled opponent would play for time, of course, observing him closely, watching for the first sign of genuine faltering, which might be merely a shift of the thumb along the foil-grip, a thrust parried a fraction of an inch in excess, a slight tensing of the fingers of the curved left hand.

Thurmond would know. Perhaps this was the enlightening death which the recondite sphinx, the Meganet Mind, had predicted for him.

Thurmond waited, smiling, alert, supremely confident. He would expect Alar to burst forward, every nerve straining to make the most of the few minutes of strong, capable fencing remaining to him before he fainted from loss of blood.

The Thief moved in and his sword leapt arrow-like in an incredibly complex body feint. But his quasi-thrust was parried by a noncommittal quasi-riposte, almost philosophical in its ambiguity. Its studied indefiniteness of statement showed that Thurmond realized to the uttermost his paramount position—that a perfect defense would win without risk.

Alar had not really expected his attack to draw blood. He merely wanted to confirm in his own mind that Thurmond realized his advantage. Most evidently he did. Simultaneously with this realization the Thief, instead of improvising a continuation of the attack, as Thurmond must expect, retreated precipitously, coughed and spat out a mouthful of hot salty fluid.

His right lung had been filling slowly. The only question was, when should he cough and void the blood? He had chosen this moment. His opponent must now take the initiative and he must be lured into overextending himself.

Thurmond laughed soundlessly and closed in with a tricky leg thrust, followed immediately with a cut across the face, both of which the Thief barely parried. But it was clear that Thurmond was not exerting himself to the fullest. He was taking no chances, because he need take none.

He could accomplish his goal in good time simply by doing nothing, or quickly if he liked, by forcing the Thief to continuous exertions. Thurmond's only necessity was to stay alive, where Alar must not only do that, but must disable his opponent as well. He could not attempt more. His oath as a Thief forbade his killing an officer of the Imperium, even in self-defense.

Without feeling despair he felt the symptoms of despair—the tightening of the throat, the vague trembling of his facial nerves, an overpowering weariness.

" 'To avoid capture or death in a situation of known factors,' " mocked Thurmond, " 'the Thief will introduce one or more new variables, generally by the conversion of a factor of relative safety into a factor of relative uncertainty.' "

At that moment Alar plumbed to the depths this extraordinary character who commanded the security forces of a hemisphere. It was a blazing, calculating intelligence that crushed opposition because it understood its opponents better than they did themselves, could silently anticipate their moves and be ready—to their short-lived astonishment—with a fatal answer.

Thurmond could quote the *Thief Combat Manual* verbatim.

Alar lowered his blade slowly. "Then it is useless to proffer my weapon in surrender, expecting you to reach for it with your left hand—"

"—and find myself sailing over your shoulder. No thanks."

"Or 'slip' in my own blood—"

"—and impale me as I rush in to finish you."

"And yet," returned the Thief, "the philosophy of safety-conversion is not limited to the obvious, rather sophomoric devices that we have just discussed, as I shall shortly demonstrate." His mouth twisted sardonically.

But only the wildest, most preposterous demand on his unearthly body would save him now. Furthermore, the thing he had in mind required that he be rid of his saber, yet safe from Thurmond for at least a moment or two.

His blade skidded across the plastic tiles toward Thurmond, who stepped back in unfeigned amazement, then tightened the grip on his own weapon and moved forward.

"The sacrifice of safety is my means of defense," continued Alar unhurriedly. "I have converted it into a variable unknown, for you are suspicious of what I shall do next. Your steps are slowing.

"You see no good reason why you can't kill me now, very quickly, but you have—shall we say, buck fever? You are curious as to what I could accomplish without my weapon that I could not accomplish with it. You wonder why I am repeatedly flexing my arms and why I do these knee bends.

"You are certain you can kill me, that all you need to do is approach and thrust your blade home. And yet you have stopped to watch, consumed with curiosity. And you are just a little afraid."

Stifling a cough, the Thief stood erect and closed his

fists tightly. There was a dry crackling sound about his clothing as he crossed the brief intervening space toward Thurmond. (Time! Time! He could make this final demand on his body, but he needed a few seconds more. It was building, building . . .)

The police minister was breathing with nervous rapidity, but stood firm.

"Don't you realize, Thurmond, that a man capable of reversing the visual process by supplying his retinal web with energy quanta can, under stress, reverse that process? That instead of furnishing electrical potential differences along afferent nerves for normal muscle activation, he can reverse the process and cause the muscles to store considerable wattage for discharge through the nerves and out the fingertips?

"Did you know that certain Brazilian eels can discharge several hundred volts—enough to electrocute frogs and fish? At my present potential I could easily kill you, but I intend to simply stun you. Since electrostatic charges escape easily from metal points, you will understand why I had to throw away my saber, even at the risk of your running me through before I could build up the necessary charge." (Enough! He now felt like a bottled bolt of lightning.)

Thurmond's blade flew up. "Come no closer!" he cried hoarsely.

The Thief paused, his bare breast six inches in front of the wavering point. "Metal is an excellent conductor," he smiled, and moved in.

The police minister jumped back, gripped his saber like a lance, took split-second aim at Alar's heart and—

Fell screaming to the floor, his writhing body wrapped in a pale blue glow. He managed to pull his pistol from his holster and to fire two shots that bounced harmlessly from Alar's Thief armor.

Then there was a brief panting pause while he glared insanely upward at his extraordinary conqueror.

Throughout his adult life he had killed, idly, nonchalantly, with no more thought or feeling than he had when he ate his breakfast or combed his hair. Some had needed killing; some hadn't. A few had been a challenge, but they died anyhow. None of that had mattered in the slightest. It had been required of those creatures only that they die. This they had done, and it was all very right, correct, and proper, for he was the master swordsman of the Imperium. But now, very suddenly, something had changed. Something had gone wrong in the ordered scheme of things. Horribly wrong. Was he, the great Giles Thurmond, about to be slain by this incompetent unknown? By this rank amateur, this contemptible tyro? Unthinkable! By the Fates, *never!* Only the equal of Thurmond could ever kill Thurmond. And there was only one equal. Which is to say . . . He raised his pistol to his head. The third shot went into his own brain.

Alar had bounded into the control room before the echo of the final shot died away. Their fight had lasted nearly forty minutes. How far had the solarion drifted?

The pyrometric gauge read 4,500 K. The temperature drop from the 5,700 degrees K of the photosphere definitely placed the solarion position in the coldest part of the sunspot—its center.

Which meant that the station must have been falling for several minutes, straight toward the sun's core.

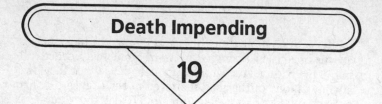

Death Impending

19

"ONE HOUR AGO," said the Meganet Mind, "their excellencies the Imperial ministers propounded a remarkable interrogatory, with the unusual requirement that I give satisfactory answers before the night is out, or die."

From where she sat with manacled ankles, Keiris examined the faces in the semicircle about her. Some were grim, some nervous, some unperturbed. With the exception of Shey and Thurmond, the whole inner council was here. In the center of them all, Haze-Gaunt, his tarsioid pet peeping fearfully over his shoulder, studied with sunken eyes the man in the transparent dome.

Even Juana-Maria was present, following the proceedings with languid curiosity from her motorchair. The Ministers of War, of Airways, of Nuclear Energy were bunched together at one end of the circle. They had been arguing in heated whispers, but sat up quickly when the Mind began to speak.

"These questions are as follows," droned the Mind. "First, were Shey and Thurmond successful in killing Alar, the Thief? If so, why have they not been heard from? Second, can Operation Finis be initiated with reasonable hope of success, even though the Alar question remains unsettled? These two questions were submitted by every member

172

of the Council, I believe. The third question—'Is Kennicot Muir alive?'—was asked by the chancellor alone."

An icy tingle began to crawl up Keiris's spine. Did the Mind really know about Kim—and Alar?

The man in the pit paused briefly, lowered his disfigured leonine head, then looked up again at the circle of faces above him. "I am able to answer your questions as follows. First—Shey and Thurmond are dead as a result of their respective attempts to destroy Alar.

"Second—the success or failure of Operation Finis is no longer dependent on the life or death of Alar, but upon an extraneous factor that will be revealed to us all within a few minutes. Thus the first two questions are answerable categorically. However, the queries concerning the existence or nonexistence of Alar and Muir can be answered only in terms of non-Aristotelian probabilities. Superficially it would appear that if Shey and Thurmond were unsuccessful, then, by definition, Alar still lives. Such a conclusion would be fallacious."

He paused for a moment and studied the intent, puzzled faces. "With the exception of her imperial majesty, all of you have spent your Aristotelian lives under the impression that 'x' is either 'A' or 'not-A.' Your conventional education has limited you to bidimensional, planar Aristotelian syllogistic classification."

"I don't follow," said Eldridge, War Minister, bluntly. "What is a planar definition and what has it to do with the existence of—of—well, say, Muir or Alar?"

"Get out your notebook and we'll draw pictures." It was Juana-Maria's dry, mocking voice. She rolled her motorchair over to him. The man pulled a leather-bound pad from his pocket somewhat hesitantly.

"Draw a circle in the middle of the sheet," directed Juana-Maria.

The mystified militarist did so. The ministers nearby craned their necks toward the pad.

"Now consider the question. Is Alar alive? As an Aristotelian you would consider only two possibilities. He's

either alive or he's dead. Thus you may write 'alive' in the
circle, and 'dead' in the space outside the circle. 'Alive' plus
'dead' then totals what the Aristotelians call a 'universe
class.' Go ahead—write them in."

Eldridge, looking a little foolish, did so.

The ironic voice continued. "But the 'dead' portion of
the card, you must remember, is defined only negatively.
We know what it is not, rather than what it is. If there are
other conditions of existence than those we are accustomed
to, that portion of the card will include them. The uncer-
tainties are infinite.

"And further, the sheet of notebook paper may be considered as a mere cross section of a sphere encompassed by
infinity. Above, below, and at angles through it are similar
cross sections in the same sphere—an infinity of them.
That is to say, by your very attempt to reduce a problem
to only two alternatives, you endow it with an infinity of
solutions."

Eldridge's face had set stubbornly. "Intending no disre-
spect, your majesty, may I submit that such considerations
are mere academic theorizing? I maintain that these two enemies of the Imperium are either alive or dead. If alive, they
must be captured and destroyed. With your permission,
your majesty, I will restate the question which was heretofore before the Mind only by implication." He addressed
the man under the dome coldly. "Is Alar, the Thief, alive?"

"Tell him if you can, then, Mind," said Juana-Maria
with a bored wave of her wrinkled hand.

"In null-Aristotelian terms," replied the Mind, "Alar is
alive. However, he has no existence in a planar Aristotelian
hypothesis, as understood by Marshal Eldridge. That is to
say, there is no person in the solar system today fitting the
fingerprints and eyeball capillary patterns in Alar's police
file."

"The same, I presume, is true for Kennicot Muir?"
asked Haze-Gaunt.

"Not precisely. Muir's identity is more diffuse. If
viewed in Eldridge's classic logic, Muir would have to be

considered as more than one man. In null-Aristotelian terms, Muir seems to have developed a certain mobility along the time axis."

"He might exist as two persons at once?" asked Juana-Maria curiously.

"Quite possibly."

Keiris listened to her own strangled voice. "Is *he*—is either of those persons—in this room—now?"

The Mind was silent for a long time. Finally he turned great sad eyes up to her. "Madame's question is surprising in view of the obvious danger to her husband if her surmise proves correct. Yet I answer as follows. One embodiment of Muir, whose existence has just been deduced by her majesty the Imperatrix in the exercise of null-Aristotelian logic, is present, but does not at the moment choose to be visible to us."

He paused and glanced at the radiochron on the wall at his left. Some of the others followed his gaze.

It was four minutes after midnight. Somewhere far above them a new day was dawning—July 21, 2177.

"However," continued the Mind, "Muir is also present in another, entirely different form, one that would be satisfactory even to Marshal Eldridge."

The ministers exchanged startled, suspicious glances.

Eldridge sprang to his feet. "Point him out!" he cried.

"The Minister for War," observed Haze-Gaunt, "is strangely naïve if he thinks the Mind is going to point out Kennicot Muir to this assembly."

"Eh?" said Eldridge. "You mean he's afraid to name him?"

"Perhaps; perhaps not. But let us see what a highly direct and specific question will bring." He turned toward the Mind and asked softly, "Can you deny that you are Kennicot Muir?"

As Alar's stunned eyes watched the pyrometer, the needle began slowly to creep up the scale, recording the fall of the station into the sunspot vortex—4,560, 4,580, 4,600.

The deeper, the hotter. Of course, the station would never reach the sun's core. The vortex would probably narrow to nothing within a thousand miles or so, in a region deep enough to have a temperature of a few million degrees. The solarion's insulative-refrigeration system could stand a top limit of 7,000.

The possibilities were several. The spot vortex might extend deep into the sun's core, with its temperature of some twenty million degrees. But even if the vortex gas stayed under 7,000 degrees all the way to the center—and he knew it could not—the station would eventually crash into the enormously dense core and burst into incandescence.

But suppose the vortex did not extend to that incredibly hot center, but, more probably, originated only a few thousand miles down? He spit out a mouthful of blood and calculated rapidly. If the spot were 16,000 miles deep the temperature at the cone apex would be a little below 7,000.

If the station would float gently to rest there, he might live for several hours before the heavy plant sank deeply enough to reach an intolerable temperature. But that wasn't going to happen. Its landing wouldn't be gentle. The station was now falling under an acceleration of twenty-seven gravities, and would probably strike the bottom of the cone at a velocity of several miles a second despite the viscosity of the spot gases. Everything about him would instantly disintegrate.

He was aware of the chair cushions pushing against his back. The metal tubing along the arms seemed considerably warmer now to his touch. His face was wet, but his mouth was dry. The thought reminded him of Captain Andrews's cache.

With nothing to do for the moment, he acted on his sudden whim. He rose, stretched himself and walked over to the wall which supported the refrigerated cabinet. He opened the door and felt the sudden wave of cool air against his perspiring face. He chuckled at an irrational thought:

why not crawl into the six cubic foot box and shut the door behind him?

He pulled out the bottle of foam and squeezed some of the thick liquid into his mouth. The sensation was extremely pleasant. He closed his eyes and for a moment imagined that Captain Andrews was next to him, saying, "It's cold and that's plenty welcome in a place like this."

He swung the door shut again on the bottle. A meaningless gesture, he thought to himself. The situation seemed so unreal. Keiris had warned him. . . .

Keiris.

Did she sense, at this moment, what he was facing?

He snorted at his own thoughts and returned to the chair.

Just precisely what did he face?

There were, indeed, several possibilities, but their conclusions were identical—a long wait, then an instantaneous, painless oblivion. He couldn't even count on an enduring, excruciating pain that might release him along the time axis, as it had done in Shey's torture room.

He became aware of a low, hollow hum, and finally traced it to the pulse at his temple. His heart was beating so fast that the individual beats were no longer detectable. The pulse had passed into the lower audio range, which meant a beat of at least twelve hundred a minute.

He almost smiled. In the face of the catastrophe that Haze-Gaunt was about to wreak on Earth, the frenzied concern of his subconscious mind for his own preservation seemed suddenly amusing.

It was then that he noticed that the room was tilted slightly. That should not be, unless the giant central gyro was slowing down. The gyro should keep the station upright in the most violent faculae and tornado prominences. A quick check of the control panel showed nothing wrong with the great stabilizer.

But the little compass gyro was turning slowly, in a very odd but strangely familiar way, which he recognized immediately. The station axis was gradually being inclined at an angle from the vertical and was rotating about its old center in a cone-like path.

The solarion was *precessing*, which meant that some unknown titanic force was attempting to invert it and was being valiantly fought off by the great central gyro.

But it was a losing battle.

He had a fleeting vision of the great station turning turtle in slow, massive grandeur. The muirium anti-grav drive overhead, now cancelling 26 of the 27 G's of the sun, would soon be beneath him, and adding to those 27 G's. Against 53 G's he would weigh some four tons. His blood would ooze from his crushed, pulpy body and spread in a thin layer over the deck.

But what could be trying to turn the station over?

The pyrometers showed almost identical convection temperatures on the sides, top and bottom, of the station— about 5,200 degrees. And radiation heat received on the sides and bottom of the plant showed about 6,900, as could be expected. But the pyrometers measuring radiation received on the upper surface of the station, which should not have exceeded 2,000 degrees—since the station surface normally was radiated only by the thin surface photosphere— showed the incredible figure of 6,800.

The station must be completely immersed in the sun. The uniform radiation on all sides proved that. Yet he was still in the sunspot vortex, as shown by the much cooler convention currents bathing the station. There was only one possible explanation. The spot vortex must be returning to the sun's surface through a gigantic U-shaped tube.

Anything going down one limb of the tube would naturally ascend the other limb inverted. The U-tube finally explained why all spots occurred in pairs and were of opposite magnetic polarity. The ionized vortex of course rotated in opposite directions in the respective limbs of the tube.

If the central gyro won out over the torrential vortex, the station *might* be swept up the other limb of the following spot twin and he *might* break the station away to safety over the penumbral edge—in which improbable event he could live as long as his punctured lung permitted, or until the storage chambers became filled with muirium and the synthesizer began turning the deadly material back into the sun to trigger a gigantic explosion.

But he could be sure that even if the station were found during that interval there would be no rescue. The discovery would be made by Imperial search vessels and the I.P.'s would simply keep the station under observation until the inevitable filling of the muirium holds.

The brooding man sat in the central operator's chair for a long time, until the steepening floor threatened to drop him out of his seat. He rose heavily to his feet and, hanging tightly to the guide rails, walked the length of the panel to a bank of huge enabling switches.

Here he unlocked the safety mechanism of the central gyro switch and pulled it out amid a protest of arcking, hissing flame. The deck immediately began to vibrate beneath him, and the rapidly increasing tilt of the floor made it difficult to stand.

The room was spinning dizzily about him as he lashed a cord to the master switch controlling the outer hatches of the muirium locks overhead. The free end he tied around his waist.

When the station turned on its back he would fall to the other end of the room and the cord attached to his lunging body would jerk open the muirium hatch switch. All the stored muirium would begin to dissolve back into its native energy quanta, the station would suddenly become a flat, gigantic space rocket and—at least theoretically—would be hurled through the rising U-limb at an unimaginable velocity.

If he were human, he would be killed instantly. If he were not human, he might survive the fantastic initial acceleration and accompany the station into the black depths of space.

The deck had almost become a vertical wall. The gyro had probably stopped and there was no turning back. For a moment he regretted his decision. At least he could have lived on a little while longer.

Always a little longer. He had squeezed out five years of life by that method. But no more. Sweat squirted from his face as, slipping and sliding, he clawed insanely at the smooth steel tiles of the deck that was now soaring over him to become the new ceiling. Then he dropped straight to what a few minutes before had been the ceiling and lay there helpless under a 53-G gravity, unable even to breathe and swiftly losing consciousness.

He knew vaguely that the rope had pulled the switches to the muirium locks, and had then broken under his enormously increased weight—that jagged fragments of his snapping ribs had pierced his heart—that he was dying.

In that instant the muirium caught. Four thousand tons of the greatest energy-giving substance ever known to man collapsed in a millisecond into a titanic space-bending shower of radiation.

He had no sensation of pain, of movement, of time, of body, of anything. But he didn't care. In his own way he was still very much alive.

Alar was dead.

And yet he knew who he was and where his destiny lay.

Armageddon

20

GODDARD, NUCLEAR MINISTER, was on his feet, staring wide-eyed alternately at the Mind and at Haze-Gaunt. "The Mind—Kennicot Muir? Impossible!"

Phelps of Airways was gripping the sides of his chair with white, trembling hands, and his fingernails were cracking and doubling back from the pressure. "How do you know it's impossible?" he shouted. "The Mind must answer that question!"

Keiris swallowed in an ecstasy of misery. She had precipitated something the Mind might not have been ready for. Thinking back, she could find no good reason for asking her question, other than intuition. But Haze-Gaunt *must* be wrong. Obviously the Mind could not be her husband. They had about the same build, but there the resemblance ended. Why, the Mind was—*ugly*. Then she stole a look at Haze-Gaunt, and lost some of her certainty.

Of the assembly, only the chancellor appeared at ease. He was reclining quietly in his plush chair, his long legs crossed casually. His perfect confidence said plainly—"I am sure of the answer and I have taken extraordinary precautions."

For Eldridge the situation was becoming unendurable. "Answer, damn you!" he cried, drawing his pistol.

Haze-Gaunt waved him back irritably. "If he is Muir, he is also an armored Thief. Put that toy away and sit down." He turned to the Mind again. "The very fact of your delay is highly revealing, but what could you hope to gain by it? A few moments more of life?" His mouth warped in the faintest of sneers. "Or doesn't the best-informed man in the system know who he is?"

Haze-Gaunt's tarsioid peeped, trembling, over his master's epaulette at the Mind, who had not changed his position. His arms rested on the arms of his chair as they had always rested. To Keiris he appeared almost as calm as usual. But Haze-Gaunt, savoring almost sensuously his victory in a generation-long struggle with the man he hated most, apparently saw something more.

"Before us, gentlemen," he observed grimly, "for all his aura of wisdom, we have a frightened animal."

"Yes, I am frightened," said the Mind, in a strong clear voice. "While we are here playing tag with identities, Toynbee Twenty-one is reeling under its death blow. If you had not forbidden all interruptions of this conference you would know that the Eastern Federation declared war on America Imperial eighty seconds ago!"

What a magnificent bluff! thought Keiris in desperate admiration.

"Gentlemen," said Haze-Gaunt, looking about him. "I trust that all of you appreciate the finer points of the Mind's latest finesse. The riddle of his identity suddenly becomes lost in the excitement of gigantic but fictitious surmises. I think we may now return to my question."

"Ask Phelps about his secret ear receptor," said the Mind coolly.

Phelps looked uncomfortable. Then he muttered: "The Mind's right—whoever he is. I have a hearing aid but it's also a radio. The Eastern Federation actually did declare war as he said."

The queer silence that followed was finally broken by Haze-Gaunt.

"This obviously changes things. The Mind will be placed under close arrest for further examination at our convenience. In the meantime the council is wasting time here. All of you have standing orders for this contingency. You will now carry them out to the letter. We stand adjourned."

He stood up. Keiris forced herself not to collapse as she relaxed.

The ministers filed out hurriedly and their footsteps and nervous whispers died away down the peristyle. The bronze elevator doors began to clang shut.

Then Haze-Gaunt turned abruptly and reseated himself. His hard eyes again fastened on the disfigured but calm face of the man in the domed pit.

Keiris's breathing grew faster. It was not over—it was just beginning.

The Mind seemed lost in a reverie, totally indifferent to the probability of imminent death.

Haze-Gaunt drew a pistol-like thing from his jacket pocket. "This is a poison-dart thrower," he said softly. "The dart can easily penetrate your plastic shell. It need only scratch you. I want you to talk about yourself and to tell me a great deal. You may begin now."

The Mind's fingers drummed indecisively on the arm of his chair. When he looked up it was not at his executioner but at Keiris. It was to her that he spoke.

"When your husband vanished ten years ago, he told you that he would contact you through me. At that time I was an obscure sideshow freak. Only in recent years have I had access to the vast literature that has brought me to my present preeminent position."

"Might I interrupt?" murmured Haze-Gaunt. "The original Meganet Mind, an obscure entertainer, had a remarkable resemblance to you. But it so happens that he died ten years ago in a circus fire. Oh, I admit that the burn tissue on your face and hands is genuine. In fact, you burned your features deliberately. With the record corrected, pray continue."

Keiris watched in fascinated horror as the Mind licked dry lips.

The Mind said, "My disguise has finally failed, then. But until now, I believe, no one suspected my identity. The wonder of it is that I was not exposed years ago. But to go on—through Keiris, I relayed vital information to the Society of Thieves, which I hoped would overthrow your rotten administration and save our civilization. But their gallant efforts are now cut short. The most brilliant minority cannot reform a disintegrating society in a bare decade."

"Then you admit that we have beaten you and your vaunted Society?" demanded Haze-Gaunt coldly.

The Mind looked at him thoughtfully. "Half an hour ago I intimated that Alar had attained a semi-godhood. Whether or not you have beaten me and my 'vaunted Society' depends on the identity of the intelligence we have been calling Alar."

"Don't hide behind words," snapped Haze-Gaunt.

"You may be able to understand me if I put it this way. In the Central Drome of the Airways Laboratories lies the recently completed *T-Twenty-two*, standing by to blast off on its maiden voyage. Five years ago, as you well know, a white-hot space ship crashed into the Ohio River and the River Police found some remarkable things. The metallic parts of the ship were identical in composition with the alloys that Gaines and I had worked out for the *T-Twenty-two*.

"Was the race of a neighboring star trying to reach our sun? We waited for further evidence. It turned up the next day when a man was found wandering along the river bank, dazed, almost naked, carrying a leather-bound book with him. The book bore the gold-stamped legend—*T-twenty-two, Log*. There is one just like it in the pilot's room of our own *T-twenty-two*."

"You weave a fine story," said Haze-Gaunt, "but we must cut it short I fear. I wanted real information, not a disjointed fairy tale." He raised the dart-pistol. The tarsioid disappeared screaming down his back.

"That man was Alar the Thief," said the Mind. "Shall I continue or do you wish to try to kill me now?"

Haze-Gaunt hesitated, then lowered the pistol. "Continue," he said.

"We kept Alar under observation in the lodgings of two Thieves, now dead. Always we held before us the possibility that he was one of your spies. The truth of his identity grew upon me only gradually, when no other explanation was possible.

"Let us look at the facts. A ship identical to the T-twenty-two landed on Earth five years ago. Yet the T-twenty-two is not due to blast off on its maiden voyage until a quarter of an hour from now. Regardless of any other facts or theory involved the ship will start moving backward in time as soon as it is launched, and will continue to move until it crashes—should I say 'crashed'?—five years ago.

"The man who shall become transformed into Alar through a geotropic response, or otherwise, and whom we might call Mr. X, will board the T-twenty-two in a few minutes with an unidentified companion, and they will be carried away in the ship at a velocity faster than that of light. Such velocities require movement backward in time, so that when Mr. X finally pilots the T-twenty-two back to Earth, he lands five years earlier than when he started. He emerges as Alar and is henceforth irrecognizable as Mr. X."

Haze-Gaunt looked at the Mind, grim-mouthed. "Do I understand that you want me to believe that someone will leave in the T-twenty-two tonight, jet backward in time, crash into the Ohio River five years ago and swim ashore as Alar?"

The Mind nodded.

"Fantastic—yet it has the elements of possibility," mused the chancellor. "Assuming for the moment that I believe you, who is the person who will enter the T-twenty-two and become Alar?"

"I'm not sure," said the Mind coolly. "He is undoubtedly someone in the metropolitan area, because the T-twenty-two jets in ten minutes. He might be—you."

Haze-Gaunt shot him a hard, calculating glance.

Keiris felt light-headed, dizzy. Haze-Gaunt become Alar? Did that account for her pseudo-recognition of the Thief? Intuitively she rejected the suggestion.

But—

"That hypothesis really becomes intriguing when we examine your relations thus far with Alar," said Haze-Gaunt. "Only a few weeks ago you yourself, with excessive modesty, warned us that Alar was the man most dangerous to the Imperial Government. After his several escapes you told us immediately where to find him and several times, through information you furnished, we nearly succeeded in killing him.

"We might be justified in concluding that you considered Alar a bitter personal enemy, a category that could easily include me—as Alar, of course—except for a serious difficulty. I have no intention of entering the *T-twenty-two*. Therefore, I am not your Mr. X, and your motive in persecuting Alar stands unexplained. I must warn you to be explicit." He raised the dart-gun again.

"An old method of teaching children to swim was to throw them in the water," said the Mind.

Haze-Gaunt looked down at him sharply. "You are suggesting that it was your intention to cause Alar to develop his remarkable gifts—whatever they are—by making it necessary that he either discover them or die. Rather a striking educational technique. But why did you suspect that he had such latent possibilities in the first place?"

"For a long time we weren't sure. Alar seemed just an ordinary man except for one thing—his heartbeat. Dr. Haven reported that Alar's heartbeat rose to the medically unheard of rate of one hundred and fifty a minute and more in times of danger. I then decided that if Alar were *homo superior* his superiority was latent. He was like a child adopted by a pack of wild animals.

"Unless he were forced to realize his superior origin, he would be doomed to run about on his metaphoric all fours for the rest of his life—with us other animals. Yet, if I could get him to his feet, he might point the way out of the devastation that is even now overwhelming us.

"So when, some six weeks ago, you were about to decide on the date of Operation Finis, I had to act, possibly prematurely. By means of unusually violent persecution, I forced Alar to develop an extraordinary photic ability, whereby he could project a scene in much the same way as a holo projector.

"Later, under the stimulus of ecstatic pain, ably administered by Shey, he became acquainted with the time axis of his four-dimensional body. Unfortunately he was unable to travel in time without this stimulus, and I can't say that I blame him for not indulging in the experience voluntarily. Yet it was an accomplishment that he had to master as we master speech—by repetition. I am certain that he finally used it again in the very act of dying on Solarion Nine.

"I next led Alar first to the moon, where he was forced to learn something of himself and the backward flight of the *T-twenty-two*, then to the sun station, with Shey and Thurmond on his trail. He *had* to emerge triumphant and fully enlightened as to his superiority and mission. The alternative was death. I gave him no choice."

Haze-Gaunt arose and began striding up and down the stone flagging, sending his pet into a chattering fright from one shoulder to the other and back again. Finally he stopped and said, "I believe you. Small wonder then that we couldn't kill Alar. On the other hand, you too must admit defeat, for your protégé seems to have abandoned both you and your cause."

"You have not understood me," the Mind said bluntly. "In Aristotelian terms, Alar is dead."

There was a shocked silence in the room that was quickly broken by two simultaneous sounds. Chancellor Haze-Gaunt burst out with, "Good!" as Madame Haze-Gaunt cried, "No!"

Keiris was collapsing slowly against the chair arm. Her

skin had so blanched that two terrible dark circles appeared under her eyes. The Mind had predicted Alar's fate, but she had never reconciled herself to it becoming a fact. There was no thought in her head that the Mind could be mistaken. No, it was true. And though the horrible realization weighed her down, she couldn't quite grasp the naked, irrefutable fact that he was dead. Alar couldn't be gone forever from their lives. No, he couldn't be gone, would never be gone. That had to be true. The Mind had said, what was it? "Alar had attained a semi-godhood." Then there was no conflict. Alar was dead and lived. Even as he lost his life, he had triumphed.

Keiris didn't fully understand, but the color began to seep back into her face.

Haze-Gaunt had paid no attention to Keiris's cry. He had permitted himself a wide grin and a smack of closed fist into open palm. Then, within seconds, he had sobered and scowled at the Mind who so imperturbably sat there and watched him.

"Then your protégé," he said, an edge of irritation creeping into his voice, "hasn't deserted you. He has merely died. Hardly a situation which should make you confident of your own success."

Somewhere behind him an elevator door opened and shut—and then there was the sound of running and stumbling feet.

It was the Minister of War, Eldridge. His uniform was disheveled and it was a darker color at the throat and armpits. Bloodshot eyes punctuated an ashen face.

Haze-Gaunt caught the man as he collapsed. "Speak, damn you!" he cried, holding the shuddering creature under the arms and shaking him.

But Eldridge's eyes merely rolled crazily and his jaw dropped a little farther. Haze-Gaunt let him fall to the floor. The War Minister moaned softly when Haze-Gaunt kicked him in the stomach.

"He was trying to tell you," observed the Mind, "that

satellites and coastal radar have picked up vast swarms of west-bound rockets This area will be utterly destroyed to a depth of several miles within five minutes."

Not a muscle in the chancellor's face changed in the long silence that followed. Even the tarsier on his shoulder seemed paralyzed.

They look like twins, thought Keiris.

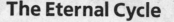
Finally, Haze-Gaunt said, rather pensively, "It is an occupational risk of the aggressor that the victim may grow impatient and strike the first blow. But this preemption of the initiative is immaterial and actually foolish, for in such event our launching areas are under standing orders to resort to total destruction patterns instead of the one-third destruction originally planned."

"Might I suggest, excellency," came the dry grave voice of Juana-Maria, who had just rolled in, "that Shimatsu has anticipated the scale of your retaliation? That his own destruction pattern for the Imperium is similarly unrestricted?"

Keiris's face slowly grew white as she watched a terrible smile-like thing transform Haze-Gaunt's mouth. But it couldn't be a smile. In the ten years she had known him he had not smiled.

He said, "That, too, was a calculated risk. So civilization must really disappear, as the Toynbeeans have so widely and fearsomely proclaimed. But I shall not remain to mourn over it. And this latest development, I believe, forcibly solves the identity of Mr. X, and hence of Alar."

He turned savagely to the Mind. "Why do you think I permitted you and your Thieves to build the *T-twenty-two*?

Research? Exploration? Bah! The weak, futile human race vanishes, but I shall escape and live! And I shall escape beyond my wildest dreams, for I shall become that invincible conqueror of time and space, Alar the Thief!"

He was sneering now at the scarred but peaceful face of the Mind. "What a simpleton you were! I know that you yourself hoped to escape in the *T-twenty-two*. That's why you had it built. And you even had a passageway, super-secret, so you thought, constructed from your dome to the *T-twenty-two* hangar. You may be interested to learn, impostor, that the tunnel has been sealed."

"I know it," smiled the Mind. "The 'secret' passageway was merely a decoy. I intend to reach the *T-22* by a much more efficient route. Since you have driven your ablest scientists underground to the Thieves, you probably have never had an adequate explanation of Thief armor. It actually consists of a field of negative acceleration and a necessary consequence is its strong repellence of rapidly approaching bodies, such as I.P. bullets.

"You probably know that acceleration is synonymous with space curvature, and the alert Haze-Gaunt intellect has now doubtless deduced the fact that this projection mechanism before me is actually capable of controlling the space surrounding anyone wearing Thief armor. In an earlier age such a phenomenon might have been called teleportation.

"Haze-Gaunt, I hope that you will not enter the *T-twenty-two*—that you will not become Alar. A few hours ago Alar recovered his memory and is by now completely integrated into an intelligence beyond our conception. In fact, it probably makes no sense to think of him as Alar any longer. If he remembered his past as you, humanity has lost its last hope. If he remembered his past as me, I think something still may be salvaged from the shambles you have made."

The orange light on the projection reader had turned a bright yellow and grew momentarily more luminous.

"The potential stored so far is sufficient to deposit me

within the pilot room of the *T-twenty-two*," said the Mind calmly, "but I must wait another thirty seconds, because this time I am taking my wife with me."

He smiled at Keiris, whose soundless lips were forming, *"Kim!"* over and over again.

"There is only one thing remaining, one thing that puzzles me," continued the Mind. "The matter of your tarsier, Haze-Gaunt—"

A low, grinding rumble rolled through the room. From somewhere came the crash of falling masonry.

The yellow pilot light on the projector flickered, then died away.

Keiris stood up in a slowly rising cloud of dust, through which she could see her husband tinkering feverishly with the teleportation machine. Juana-Maria had her handkerchief to her mouth and was blinking her eyes wildly. Haze-Gaunt coughed, then spat and looked about for Keiris. She gasped and hobbled backward a step.

Then several things happened at once. Haze-Gaunt leaped toward her, tossed her dizzily over his shoulder, then faced Kennicot Muir—the Meganet Mind—who had burst through the door of the plastic dome.

The great man seemed to fill the room.

Haze-Gaunt shrank away, with Keiris on one shoulder and the tarsier on the other. "I'll shoot you if you move!" he shouted at Muir, waving his dart-pistol. He began to back toward the elevators.

Keiris, remembering the deaths of Gaines and Haven, tried desperately to voice a similar warning, but her voice was paralyzed. She managed to loosen and drop her right sandal, and the long toes of her right foot were closing around the long knife in her thigh scabbard when Muir replied:

"I am immune to the poison. I developed it myself. Therefore, I will accompany you down your private, battery-operated elevator. I don't believe the others—"

He was interrupted by a high-pitched, terrified chattering. It was the tarsier, who had scrambled down the chancellor's leg and was trying vainly to halt the man by clutching at both legs.

"*Don't go! Don't go!*" it cried in a tiny, inhuman voice. It was the most chilling sound Keiris had ever heard. The beastling had joined the drama as a full-fledged member of the troupe, with lines to speak, and a death to die. Little creature, she thought, *who are you?*

Haze-Gaunt said something under his breath. His leg flung out. The little animal sailed through the air and crashed into the marbled wall. It lay motionless where it fell, with its body bent backward queerly.

Muir was running swiftly toward them when Haze-Gaunt cried, "Is your wife immune?"

Muir stopped precipitately. Haze-Gaunt, grinning viciously, continued his deliberate retreat toward his elevator door.

Keiris craned her neck from her awkward and painful position and looked at her husband. The anguish on his face turned her heart to water. It was the first time in ten years that his fire-born disguise had relaxed its frozen, toneless immobility.

The elevator doors opened. Haze-Gaunt carried her inside.

"It is finished," groaned Muir. "So *he* is Alar. I let you suffer ten years for this—my poor darling—poor humanity." His voice was unrecognizable.

In her awkward position Keiris could not inflict a vital wound on Haze-Gaunt. She knew then what she must do.

The elevator door was closing as she heaved herself sideways off Haze-Gaunt's shoulder. The weight of her body twisted his arm and she dropped across the doorway. As she fell, she cried, "*He is not Alar!*"

Her knee doubled under her and the knife between her toes flashed in the light. She dropped heavily upon the upturned blade, driving it into her heart.

The woman's body had blocked the sliding panel.

Haze-Gaunt tugged the corpse frantically into the elevator as there was a blur of movement toward him.

The elevator door clanged shut, and Juana-Maria was alone in the room.

The three of them, Kennicot Muir, Haze-Gaunt, and Keiris, the living and the newly dead, were joined in their own weird destiny and had left her to hers.

For a long time the fine brown eyes were lost in thought. Her revery was finally penetrated by a shrill, painful piping.

The tarsioid, despite its broken back, was still breathing limply, and its eloquent saucer-like eyes were turned up pleadingly to her. Their piteous message was unmistakable.

Juana-Maria reached into the side pocket of her chair and found the syringe and vial of analgesic. Then she hesitated. To kill the little beast would perilously deplete the vial. There would be pain enough for herself in the next few minutes. Damn Haze-Gaunt anyway. Always bungled his murders.

She filled the syringe quickly, rolled the chair over to the little creature, bent over slowly to pick it up.

The injection was done quickly.

She retracted the needle and the dying animal lay raglike in her lap, staring at her face with fast-glazing eyes. And then she knew it was dead and that she was exhausted. The titular ruler of one and a half billion souls could not even move her own hands. The syringe dropped to the tiles and shattered.

How easy now to slide into an unwaking revery, forever. So Muir was to become Alar and attain something akin to immortality. That was just. It seemed to her that the man was simply following a natural development to its logical conclusion. And by the same token Haze-Gaunt would have to change, too.

She wondered what Muir-Alar could do that would avoid Operation Finis. Perhaps he would go back in time and cause Haze-Gaunt to be still-born. But then another dictator, even more ruthless, might arise and destroy civilization. Of course, the god-man might prevent Muir from discovering muirium, or even stop the classic nuclear physicists, Hahn, Meisner, Fermi, Oppenheimer and the rest, from splitting the uranium atom.

But she suspected the discoveries would be made in due time by others. Perhaps the Michelson-Morley experiment, which had proved the contraction of matter in its line of motion and started Einstein off on his theory of the equivalence of matter and energy, could be doctored so that Michelson would actually get the interference image he sought.

But then there would be Rutherford's work on the suspiciously heavy electrons, and an infinity of allied research. And human nature being what it was, it would again be just a question of time.

No, the main difficulty would be in the mind of man. He was the only mammal hell-bent on exterminating his own species.

She was glad it was not her task to humanize humanity or to be a god-mother to Toynbee Twenty-two.

She peered down at the furry lump in her lap and wondered if Muir had ever divined its identity. Perhaps she alone understood.

Two living beings would emerge from the ship when the trip had ended. Kennicot Muir would by then have evolved into Alar. The other would be Haze-Gaunt—a changed Haze-Gaunt . . . All as predicted by John Haven's Geotropic Project. When two specimens are subjected to speeds faster than light, one evolves, the other devolves.

The darkened chamber was slowly whirling around and around. She could no longer move her lips, but she could move her eyes to stare at the tiny corpse of the tarsier. With a great effort she marshaled her last clear thought:

"Poor Haze-Gaunt. Poor tiny animal Haze-Gaunt. To think that *you* always wanted to finish killing *me*."

A moment later the chamber was vaporized.

THE LEADER, GRAY, grizzled and cold-eyed, paused and sniffed the air moving up the valley. The old Neandertal smelled reindeer blood a few hundred yards down the draw, and also another unknown smell, like, yet unlike, the noisome blend of grime, sweat and dung that characterized his own band.

He turned to his little group and shook his flint-tipped spear to show that the spoor had been struck. The other men held their spears up, signifying that they understood and they would follow silently. The women faded into the sparse shrubbery of the valley slope.

The men followed the reindeer path on down the gully, and within a few minutes peered through a thicket at an old male Eoanthropus, three females of assorted ages and two children, all lying curled stuporously under a windfall of branches and debris that overhung the gully bank.

Blood still drained sluggishly from a half-devoured reindeer carcass lying under the old man's head.

Some sixth sense warned Eoanthropus of danger. He shook his five hundred pound body and convulsed into a snarling squat over the reindeer, searching through nearsighted eyes for the interlopers. The females and children scurried behind him with mingled fear and curiosity.

"All men are brothers!" shouted the aging Neandertaler. "We come in peace and we are hungry."

He dropped his spear and held up both hands, palms outward.

Eoanthropus clenched his fists nervously and squinted uncertainly toward his unwelcome guests. He growled a command to his little family, and like shadows they melted up the side of the draw. And after hurling a final imprecation at the invaders, the old male scuttled up the hill himself.

The hunters watched the group vanish, and then two of them ran toward the reindeer carcass with drawn flint knives. With silent expert strokes they cut away the hind quarters of the animal and then looked up inquiringly at the old leader.

"Take no more," he warned. "Reindeer may be scarce here, and *they* may have to come back or go hungry." He could not know that the genes of his fathers had been genetically reengineered by an inconceivably titanic intelligence, with the consequence that the colloidal webs in his frontal lobes had been subtly altered. And he could neither anticipate nor visualize the encounter of his own descendants in the distant future with their Cro-Magnon cousins, the tall people who would move up from Africa across the Sicilo-Italian land bridge.

He had no way of knowing that even as he had spared the animal-like Eoanthropus, so would he, Neandertal, be spared by Cro-Magnon. Nor had he any way of knowing that by offering the open palm instead of the hurled spear he had changed the destiny of all mankind to come. Or that he had dissolved, by preventing the sequence of events that led to its formation, the very intelligence that had wrought this marvelous change in the dawn-mind.

For the entity sometime known as Muir-Alar had rejoined Keiris in a final eternity, even as the Neandertal's harsh vocal cords were forming the cry that would herald the eventual spread of Toynbee Twenty-two throughout the universe:

"All men are brothers!"

Afterword: The Flight Into Tomorrow

By Brian W. Aldiss

As LONG AS there is no general agreement on what does or does not constitute science fiction, there can be no agreement as to what "pure" science fiction is, although the term is frequently used. But Charles Harness's *The Paradox Men* must come close to anybody's idea of one kind of pure science fiction: the wild and imaginative kind which juggles amusedly with many scientific concepts.

Before this imaginative play is dismissed as fantasy—or perhaps "fancy," in S. T. Coleridge's definition—it is wise to consider how Harness has been moved by the tremendous challenge of Einstein's theories of Relativity. The American philosopher Henry LeRoy Finch says of Einstein's imagination that it "reformed our conception of the universe." The original formulation of the Special Theory of Relativity involved an imaginative feat unparalleled in human thought. . . . When asked many years later how he had come to formulate this theory, Einstein is said to have replied: "By refusing to accept an axiom."*

The magazine SF writers of the thirties and forties were fired by this defiance of intellectual frontiers. They came,

---

*Henry LeRoy Finch: Introduction to *Conversation with Einstein*, by Alexander Nosekowski, USA, 1970.

paradoxically, to feel that one was being most true to the spirit of science by upsetting all its established laws which, like stones, might conceal a real truth beneath them. In the same way, another influential thinker of the age, Sigmund Freud, generated disciples who were moved to scrutinize words and actions for their concealed motives, often turning meaning upside down in the process.

This contemporary preoccupation which "calls all in doubt" extended to questioning some of the basic tenets upon which Western civilization is based. Two such tenets are questioned.

First, Harness contradicts the conventional idea of civilization as a neat progression. To this end, he employs the theory of Arnold Toynbee, whose multi-volume *A Study of History* was then highly fashionable, that civilization was not the continual if faltering upward march as depicted by H. G. Wells in his book *The Outline of History,* and by many other historiographers before and since, but rather cyclic in nature, somewhat as proposed by Oswald Spengler, each civilization containing the seeds of its eventual decline. Harness proposes a spaceship which will act as a bridge between Western civilization and its successor civilization, setting the main action of the novel in the heady days of Western decadence, when Imperatrix Juana-Maria of the House of Chatham-Perez rules over the Western Hemisphere.

The second basic tenet brought to question is the Aristotelian logic on which our rational thinking has been based since the Renaissance. The Greeks formulated a concise way of handling concepts in which the answer at each stage of an argument was negative or positive (Yes or No); as long as this problem is settled at each stage, the deductive series can continue ever onwards. With the immensely greater information-flow about us today, we require more ways of solving problems (intuition must play its part, for instance); Harness's non-Aristotelians are simply people who use new deductive processes. Nowadays, we might call them lateral thinkers. The challenge to Aristotelian logic was a popular one in the science fiction magazines when Harness was writing; it helped reinforce the idea, derived from Einstein, that anything was possible in an impossible universe. It is most notably enshrined in A. E. Van Vogt's two novels and titles, *The World of Null-A* and *The Pawns of Null-A*.

Incorporating all these elements of change, the novel is itself about a world of change, in which eventually all men become brothers.

Some years ago, I categorized this novel and others like it—such as the Van Vogt titles already mentioned—as Widescreen Baroque. The label remains adequate. Despite the intellectual background sketched above, *The Paradox Men* is far from being a work of cerebration; indeed, it is a fast-paced pursuit story. Its style is exuberant rather than fine, sometimes dropping into extravagance—which is one definition of baroque. Widescreen Baroque requires at least the whole solar system for its setting, with space- and preferably time-travel as accessories, and a complex plot with mysteries and lost identities and a world to ransom. Perspectives between Possible and Impossible must be foreshortened dramatically; great hopes must mingle with terrible destruction. Ideally, the characters involved should have short names and short lives.

All these conditions are fulfilled by Harness's novel. The hero, Alar the Thief, is a secret master, a traveler through many dimensions, a cryptogram in the riddle of his culture, and he dies before the conclusion of the novel.

Most Widescreen Baroque novels are ultimately frivolous. Under all the swashbuckle, there is a pleasing seriousness about *The Paradox Men*, a seriousness having nothing to do with the ideas of Toynbee or Einstein, which act in part as window-dressing. For all the surrealist effects—of which the plunge into the raging heart of the sun is the most spectacular—for all the derring-do and costume drama, Harness is saying something about life. Though his statement is never set directly into words, it is far from vague; on the contrary, it is clear and concise. That living is vital is hardly a profound message, yet it was profound and immediate enough to move the great Elizabethan and Jacobean dramatists. Their feeling for "this sensible warm motion" was most aptly expressed when set against torture and death, and Harness's lively figures move against that same dark foil: "The Thief knelt without a word and gently gathered Haven's body into his arms. The body of the older man seemed curiously shriveled and small. Only now did Alar realize what stature the bare fact of being alive contributed to flesh and bone." (But Alar himself will undergo death and transfiguration.)

And the woman Keiris, who loves Alar, endures as much suffering as Webster's Duchess of Malfi, and surely discovers that "death hath ten thousand several doors for men to take their exits." This is very much a neo-Jacobean novel, right down to the profusion of grand gestures and adjectives.

Charles Harness was born in Texas in 1915. He is also known for a short mystic novel, *The Rose,* again on a theme of death and transfiguration, and for a fantastic novel, *The Ring of Ritornel,* which employs the same theme against a galactic background, with eternity represented as a recurrent cycle of cosmic death and rebirth. Each of Harness's infrequent but highly individual novels enjoys a coterie reputation. In the case of *The Paradox Men,* there is every reason to believe that that reputation will continue to grow.

I WAS BORN in 1915 in Colorado City, a little town in West Texas. (It sprang up in 1870 when the railroad came in and the Comanches left.) The area was (and is) dry, bleak, semisavage, wholly beautiful. We lived at "Riverside," a few miles outside the town, on the Colorado River, surrounded by mesquite, cactus, and sandstorms. Mother tried to grow honeysuckle on an "arbor." It laughed forlornly and died. (Here in Maryland it's a victorious weed.) Centipedes were five inches long. Shake out your shoes every morning to make sure thay harbored no "stingin' lizards" (scorpions). My big brother Billy was an artist; he sketched water moccasins wreathed languidly in the river brambles. My older sister and I bounced rubber balls against the sunny side of the house, trying to hit tarantulas that had crawled up on the warm cinder blocks. These memories have led to stories about spiders: Raq, in *The Ring of Ritornel*; the aliens in *The Araqnid Window*; Atropos, in *The Venetian Court*. Some evenings Dad would stand on the front porch, looking at the western sky, wondering if that ominous black cloud would drop a funnel, or at other times listening to the woman screaming upriver. Except, he explained, it wasn't a woman, it was a panther, and "you kids had better sleep inside tonight."

Alas, all that came to an end. We moved to Fort Worth. During my boyhood there I got interested in chemistry and radio. My pals and I had a chem lab in a backyard shack. Initiation was by exposure to burning sulfur in the closed shack. If you could last five minutes (by guess—nobody had a watch), you were a member. Radio: I built a crystal set, then a one-tube set. We bought no parts. Everything was scrounged, salvaged, borrowed. We didn't even have earphones. We used an old telephone receiver we found in a vacant house. First reception: *Tiptoe through the Tulips*. I can still hear it. We broadcast, too, using an old Ford spark coil as oscillator. Morse code only, of course. The best time for this was Saturday afternoons, when the TCU football games were being broadcast. The spark coil covered the entire electromagnetic band, and neighborhood response was terrific. We were exuberant little wretches.

In high school I coedited the school paper with William Barney, subsequently Texas poet laureate. Also in high school I tried my hand at short stories because (a) my brother Billy wrote short stories in his English class at TCU and (b) to see whether I could (I couldn't) and (c) because my journalism teacher was giving a course in short story writing. At the end of her course we published our own anthology. A lot of short stories were being published in the "slicks" in those days: *The Saturday Evening Post, Colliers, Liberty* . . . All gone now, except a highly modified *Post*.

And so in Fort Worth I finished high school and got my first full-time job (in a paper warehouse—in the red light district). Simultaneously I attended TCU's night school on a ministerial scholarship. This arrangement stemmed from a mix of factors. Firstly, because we were poor, and it was the only way I could get into college. Also, I had (then) a genuine piety and associated Christian convictions: genetic traits passed down from early Harness ancestors. (My great uncle George, several generations back, had such idealism and trust in his fellow man that he built his cabin on an Iroquois warpath. This was grave doctrinal error.)

Later I got a job as a fingerprint clerk in the Fort Worth police department, and in that capacity I had the pleasure of keeping in touch with old friends from both district and seminary. I have tried to recapture some of these happy earthy times of serail and jail in *Redworld*, an SF novel that will probably never be published. (One very nice lady editor had a superlative for it, though: "Most disgusting thing I ever read.")

Billy died of inoperable brain tumors when he was twenty-six. He's a major character in several of my novels: Ruy Jacques in *The Rose*, Omere in *The Ring of Ritornel*, and himself in *The Catalyst*. The last line in *The Paradox Men* is a salute to Billy.

But on to Washington, D.C., and ten years with the U.S. Government. There I married Nell White, the prettiest and smartest girl in my high school class and my college sweetheart. In Washington I got a B.S. in chemistry, then an Ll.B. (both from George Washington University), became a patent lawyer, and a father. Nell and I have two grown children and one grandchild. They live nearby and we see them frequently.

I've been fascinated by SF and fantasy ever since the mid-twenties, when Billy started bringing in copies of *Amazing Stories*, *Weird Tales*, and *Argosy*. Later I added *Astounding*, *Unknown*, *Startling*, *Thrilling Wonder*, *Planet*, and others. I wrote my first story (charitably bought by *Astounding* in 1947) because I needed the money. (Red ink is a great stimulant.)

I worked full time as a patent attorney for thirty-five years, and I've written SF sporadically during that time. But now I've retired, and maybe it's time to quit writing. And I will, as soon as I come to a good stopping place.

Charles L. Harness

March 1984